Meeting at Matthew Street

Lisa Kirkman

CONTACT LISA

To book Lisa Kirkman for corporate events
contact her through
www.MeetingAtMatthewStreet.com

© 2020 by Lisa Kirkman
2nd Edition
www.MeetingAtMatthewStreet.com

Cover design by Alea Kittell

All rights reserved. No part of this publication may be reproduced, stored in a retrieval system, or transmitted, in any form or by any means, electronic, mechanical, photocopying, recording or otherwise without the prior permission of both the copyright owner and the publisher.

This book is a work of fiction. All the characters, organizations and events in this book are either products of the author's imagination
or are used strictly for fictional purposes. Any resemblance to actual persons living or dead are purely coincidental and references
to actual persons were done solely as a means of conveying a fictional story and did not actually occur.

For my husband Phillip Kittell,
who believes in me, supports
what I do, and always encourages me.
And to my readers…
Be praus*.

*Praus

you'll have to read the book to know what that means.

TABLE OF CONTENTS

CHAPTER ONE	1
CHAPTER TWO	14
CHAPTER THREE	21
CHAPTER FOUR	27
CHAPTER FIVE	30
CHAPTER SIX	34
CHAPTER SEVEN	42
CHAPTER EIGHT	50
CHAPTER NINE	55
CHAPTER TEN	65
CHAPTER ELEVEN	68
CHAPTER TWELVE	76
CHAPTER THIRTEEN	81
CHAPTER FOURTEEN	88
CHAPTER FIFTEEN	102
CHAPTER SIXTEEN	106
CHAPTER SEVENTEEN	119
CHAPTER EIGHTEEN	122
CHAPTER NINETEEN	126
CHAPTER TWENTY	131
CHAPTER TWENTY-ONE	147
CHAPTER TWENTY-TWO	154
CHAPTER TWENTY-THREE	156

CHAPTER TWENTY-FOUR	166
CHAPTER TWENTY-FIVE	177
CHAPTER TWENTY-SIX	178
CHAPTER TWENTY-SEVEN	185
RECIPES	193
LIBBY'S SAUSAGE CORNBREAD	194
JERRY'S EASY OVEN ROUX - CHICKEN GUMBO	195
AMOS'S INDIAN CURRY AND MANGO CHICKEN	197
ACKNOWLEDGEMENTS	199
SOURCE NOTES	201
ABOUT THE AUTHOR	202
REVIEWS	203

Lisa Kirkman

CHAPTER ONE

"Wake up!" the interrogator shouted while slapping Marcus across his right cheek with the back of his hand. "We're not done here," he said with disgust. He was getting absolutely nowhere with his interrogation and he was getting tired even though he had a full night's sleep. That certainly couldn't have been said for his prisoner. He had not been allowed to sleep for days. Backing away from Marcus who was handcuffed to the arm of a heavy chair, the interrogator propped himself on the edge of the table positioned directly across from Marcus. He crossed his arms and looked down upon the forty year old man that he had been browbeating unsuccessfully for days and shook his head. He inspected the now degraded sight sitting before him. The disheveled hair. The sweat beaded brow. Despite his stocky build, Marcus's neck no longer had the strength to support his head upright and it wobbled either all the way forward or all the way back like a ball on a string.

The room they were in was small and drab. It was void of any notable distinction. Nothing hung on the walls and the decorator, if there had ever been one, must have liked working with an all grey color pallet, as if the room had taken a black and white photo of itself, negating all previous signs of color it may have once contained. Other than the straight backed chair that Marcus was being detained in, a card sized table with thick metal legs took center stage to the room. A small digital recorder sat on the far corner across from a thick metal pipe which was bolted to the top of the table. This was where some detainees had at times been handcuffed to the table top instead of the chair. The interrogator didn't care for that method, however. He liked to keep some space between him and the person he was questioning. That gave him control over his own personal space.

"Your breath stinks," he once told a client. He liked the word "client." It sounded so business-like and professional. It made him feel like the attorney that he had once aspired to become.

Across the table from the detainee was a broken chair meant for the interrogator to sit in which sat on only four of its five casters. The fifth didn't touch the ground until you shifted your weight. Then it would make a trade with one of the other casters as it in turn lost contact with the bare floor underneath. It was a typical government issued chair. He figured it probably cost 60 bucks, but was sold to the agency for $600 each by some politician's son. To make the chair add insult to potential injury, literally, it sprang wildly with a broken back rest that if you leaned back in it too far, you'd end up falling fully backwards. It made the interrogator wonder who was being broken here, the employees or the detainees – excuse me, "clients?"

While looking down on Marcus, he crossed his right ankle over his left and bounced his knee to release some of the tension he was fighting. He studied Marcus for a moment longer in frustration. With the tip of his tongue he felt at a piece of sausage stuck between two molars, while he contemplated his next move. He raised a hand to his face and rubbed at the stubble of his chin…huh!...he'd missed a spot…then he inhaled deeply, pursed his lips and let his breath escape with a blast before asking for the millionth time. "Where are you from?"

Marcus couldn't even comprehend the question. It sounded more like an old vinyl record being run backward at a slow speed. Hours before, he still had presence of mind to ask himself, "How many days? How many days had gone by with these interrogations?" Marcus tried early on to gauge the time by the clothing that the inquisitors were wearing, and by the changing of the shifts; to determine how many days they'd kept him awake with questioning. But after days of sleep deprivation it was all a blur. He'd lost track of time, location, why he was there, and all things that led up to his horrific fate. He struggled to raise his head toward the interrogator looming over him. The harsh light positioned above and behind him cast elongated, macabre shadows over the interrogator's face making his nose appear almost beak-like. In his weakened state this was enough to trigger a hallucination which morphed the interrogator into a witchy old hag. Marcus recoiled briefly from the sight, but this simple act of looking up sent his head spinning. Dizzily, the room took several revolutions before his eyes and Marcus exploded in a burst of hysterical sobs. When the room slowly came to a halt his sobbing turned to uncontrollable laughter. He couldn't stop laughing. His ribs started to hurt. Or was he crying? He couldn't tell. Was it even his own voice he heard as the sound compounded upon itself over and over again creating a cacophony of echoes inside his head? Or was the laughter coming from somewhere far off?

He struggled to listen more intently and was finally able to discern that the distant laughter he was hearing

MEETING AT MATTHEW STREET

was that of the sweet, gentle tones of his wife's voice. She was laughing as he gave her a huge bear hug and spun her around kicking up a light brown dust beneath their feet while she plead between giggles to be put down. She beat on his shoulders with playful fists saying that she had chores to do and he was keeping her from them with his silliness. His dear wife. She was always working to take the best care of their family. Oh, how he missed her. He stopped spinning her around, lowering her gently to her bare feet.

He longed to stay this way for eternity, seeing her as he once did, feeling the joy of her arms around him, the touch of love from another human being. He looked into her eyes with great awe because for the first time in ages he was able to make out all the fine details. The intimate details that he had long since forgotten. The nuances that time had erased, but that his now tortured mind unlocked briefly. Every fleck, every starburst, every glimmer was revealed in crystal clarity to him, drawing him deeper into sheer bliss.

But then his reverie was abruptly shattered by the sound of a gruff voice that tore him away from this most precious moment that he was entertaining deep within his mind.

"Where are you from?" The interrogator asked again.

Marcus looked back again into the longing eyes of his wife one last time as she pulled away from him. He grabbed for her arm and as it slipped down the length of his own, he watched her image fade away until the tips of their fingers touched one final time. Her form disintegrated into a grey mist that merged and became one with the grey walls of the room. He looked at the tip of his finger, still feeling the lingering sensation of her touch. With heartbreak in his voice, now broken, he began to speak in the tongue of his youth. In Aramaic he said sadly, "I'm from the outskirts of Jerusalem."

"Damn it!" the interrogator cursed causing Marcus to jump in his seat. "Don't tell me I'm gonna have to get a gawdamned interpreter. In English, shit head. In English! Where are you from?!"

Marcus squirmed in his seat while his mind put forth yet another hallucination. This one made it appear that he was locked in a room located in the bowels of the Church of Saint-Jacques. It reeked of body odor and mildew. Huddled within the stone walled room were a group of clergymen wearing black cloaks over white habits who hovered piously over him with looks of disgust on their pompous faces. Marcus answered his inquisitor's question resentfully, "I'm from the outskirts of Jerusalem," he said, but this time it was answered in perfect 13th century French.

"In English!" came the response to this latest reply.

"I'm from the outskirts of Jerusalem," Marcus replied, defeated and deflated, with no discernable accent in the language that his interrogator had been demanding of him.

"*Finally*! We're getting somewhere," the interrogator said jumping up quickly to make sure that his digital recorder was working properly. "You're doin' great Marcus. A few more questions and you'll be given a pillow and a soft bed. Now tell me from the beginning who the hell you are." Pulling the chair up with a clatter, he took a seat on the opposite side of the table and leaned as if poised to pounce upon every word that would soon be spoken. His elbows rested on the top of the table, his chin was propped at the pinnacle of his clasped hands. He gave his full attention to what was about to be conveyed. To look at him, he was like a schoolgirl revealing a crush on her science teacher, but there was one exception. His admiration wasn't for Marcus, but for himself. It was full-on, self-centered satisfaction that he was reveling in. With pride he knew he'd just broken through while others hadn't and he was getting ready to take the questioning to the next level. He was "the man!" No one was as successful as he was in the interrogation room and this guy had definitely been the toughest he'd ever come across, hands down!

As if watching a movie, Marcus began to describe what he was now visualizing in his mind's eye. Slurring his words and under the control of a brain fog that had him half asleep, he proceeded. "I'm in my shop and a customer is asking for a ceremonial jar...30 gallons. He said mine are known for being the best," Marcus said while waving his hand palm up, making his handcuffs rattle against the chair's arm. The noise of the restraint briefly distracted him from his recount and he looked down at his cuffed wrist, turning his palm first upward and then down, observing the back of his hand with bewildered curiosity at the metal contraption fashioned around his wrist.

The interrogator worried that his train of thought was being compromised by the distraction.

"Keep going. You're in your shop," he gently directed him back to his statement.

"He wants a ceremonial jar and he has been sent by Annas to obtain one. I'm flattered, but I tell him I'm really not feeling well and I can't commit to a timeframe for completion. I will see if my son can complete the order, but the man won't accept this. I assure him my son is more than competent and skilled at producing the jar that he's requesting, but he *won't* hear of it. Annas says it *must* be made by my hands and *my* hands only. That's when I realize he is no longer requesting, but more like threatening me to fulfill his order. I'm scared for my family, so I do the best that I can do, but I am already *so* ill and weak. The harder I work to complete the order, the weaker I get. I'm trying, but...but... I tried!" Marcus shouted and began to cry again. "Ahhh...." he cried out in great anguish. Clearly the sleep deprivation had him emotional beyond his control. So distraught was he that drool hung from his lips and snot began to creep from one nostril as he kept repeating through heavy tears, "I tried!!!" The sobbing wracked his body and went on for what seemed like a full minute as Marcus choked on his own words to continue further.

"I tried to work, but I was so sick and soon I could no longer rise from my pallet. I was totally bedridden and after two more days I could feel my essence leaving my body in waves as my wife, daughter and four sons looked on. I had been ill for weeks, and this was clearly now the end. My eldest son comforted my beloved wife and in the corner of the room I saw angels going up and down a rope. They were calling for me to go with them. I didn't want to worry my family by leaving them, but the angels said it was OK, so I finally agreed to join them." Marcus let out a breath that ended in a gurgle.

The interrogator flattened his palms on the table and poised himself to jump up and resuscitate Marcus. This was not his first time to hear a death rattle while interrogating a person of interest. But Marcus's chest soon inflated with a great heave and he continued.

"As soon as I agreed to join the angels, I found myself immediately floating above everything in the room, looking down from the height of the ceiling at my family who were surrounding my body. But I knew that was no longer me that I was looking at because *I* was floating above them. I watched my wife as she threw herself across my body and began to wail pitifully. But I felt nothing but peace, comfort and no sorrow at all.... just a curiosity at the scene as it unfolded below. I then floated through the roof and saw neighbors, councilmen and customers all gathered outside my house. I could hear them as they began to murmur amongst themselves with news that I had just died. As I continued to rise I could hear the sound of air passing by my ears as I ascended higher and higher. When I turned to see where I was headed, I saw a brilliant light that shone in front of me brighter than any kiln fire I'd ever built. If colors could have emotions, this light was the color of love. It's hard to explain. It was a light and it was a feeling all at the same time."

"I was soon in heaven. The colors were *astounding*! Colors that aren't possible on earth. Sooo pretty!" He gasped at the memory and for the first time in days, his weakened, sleep deprived body seemed to revive. His lifeless glazed eyes began to twinkle as his head turned from side to side taking in the glory of his hallucination. "I could 'think' myself anywhere I wanted to go. A faraway planet, a breathtaking mountain top... there was nowhere that I couldn't *think* myself to. I was so very very happy." He paused, and then looked sorrowful, "But then I was told my time to be there had not yet come and that a place had not been prepared for me yet."

With a jerk of his restrained hands as if there had been an explosion he continued, "Then there was darkness and a huge crash of thunder." Marcus grasped the arms of his chair as he spoke. "The ground shook beneath me and I awoke with a gasp of air in my lungs and found myself laying in my family's burial tomb. There was beautiful music everywhere and multiple voices were happily calling out to God." The slight give of his handcuffs allowed him to feel the clothing on his torso and chest as he looked down at his body. "I was covered in a shroud and spices. I struggled to pull these coverings aside and when I walked out, I found others like me. Wincing he said, "We were blinded by a glowing light because our eyes were sensitive and needed to adjust. Our limbs were wobbly like a newborn calf," he chuckled a bit. "As my surroundings came into focus I was able to discern who the others were that were near me. There was my mother, long deceased, my father and a brother who had died at 3 years of age more than 25 years earlier. We were all so confused we didn't even greet each other at first." His brow furrowed and he shook his head slightly in dismay. "Why were we suddenly here? Why did we come back to life?"

At that moment the interrogator slammed his palms on the table, stood up and kicked the chair backwards with a loud rattle of casters across the floor. It hit the wall behind him and tipped over with a clang. He started to pace the tiny room in large strides.

Marcus continued without being affected by the commotion. "As people from the town saw us, some screamed and ran away in fear," he said as if that would only be natural. "Others ran toward us, hugging us with tears of joy." He shrugged his shoulders, "My revived family members and I didn't know what to do, so we stumbled our way toward the home I had lived in before my passing."

"Enough!" Shouted the interrogator as he lunged toward the table and slammed his fist down on top of the digital recorder with one hand and swept it away with the other, slinging it across the table and into the nearby wall. It landed on the floor in pieces, the back had come loose and batteries spun away in multiple directions. He walked to the door and threw it open. The door's handle left an indentation in the wall where the two came into contact. In a rage the interrogator walked several doors down the hallway and into the office of his boss to report what had just happened. Upon entering his boss' office he blasted, "Shit! Shit! *Shit!*"

"What?" His boss asked with surprise looking up from his paperwork. He'd never seen his colleague so angry.

"Marcus finally gave a statement but he's been pushed too far. Nothing but bullshit. Pure bullshit! Some fantasy story straight out of a Stephen King novel. Damn! What a waste. We didn't get a damn thing from that son of a bitch. What the *hell* is his story? Damn it!"

The boss reached over for his phone, picked up the receiver and said, "It's ok. We'll give it a go in a few days. I'll call for an escort back to holding. Just calm down and go write up your report. We'll see if we can get another method approved, but in the meantime we'll see if he talks in his sleep or gives us any usable info in his cell.

Lisa Kirkman

Maybe put a roommate in with him that he'll talk to. Just chill out Stellman. We'll get it. He'll break."

The interrogator turned to leave but not before slamming his open palm on the doorframe in anger. A framed photo of his boss standing with a political activist named Viktor Hoven, and the director of the CIA consequently was jarred from its nail and slid down the wall to the floor with a crash. A fourth man could be made out under the now crazed glass of the framed photo. He was unfamiliar to most people. Most would not know that his claim to fame, allowing him to be included with the others who were pictured golfing that day, was that he was the wealthy brother of a long term U.S. Senator. Other than his connections, he was just a useful idiot that Viktor Hoven liked to run his shady deals through.

"Such a waste of time. Zombie bullshit story!" Stellman cursed under his breath while exiting, completely ignoring the fallen photo he had just broken.

He went to the break room and poured a cup of coffee, loaded it up with sugar and the powdered crap that they had in there. "Why couldn't they spring for some flavored creamer from one of those frickin' pump things? You don't even have to refrigerate that shit. No telling what's in it, but it's better than this gritty, tasteless powder." He thought. Nothing was going right. "Can't even get a decent cup of coffee for heaven's sake." He finished stirring the creamer in his cup and aggressively tossed the stir stick in the trash as he left the break room. It missed and ricocheted to the floor.

"Screw it!" he thought looking down at the stick laying on the floor while not looking where he was going. Subsequently, as he exited the break room he almost walked head-on into a well-groomed man passing by in the hallway. As a result, he managed to spill some of his coffee on his shoe and down one pants leg. Great! Could the day get any worse? "Son of a bitch!"

Stellman quickly returned to the break room to wet a fist full of brown paper towels and try to save his pants from the creamer stains.

The man he had almost run into in the hall leaned inside the door and inquired, "Do you happen to know where Marcus Cain is?"

Not even looking up, Stellman continued dabbing at his pants with his right hand and gestured with the other toward the other end of the building, telling him that he was in room 402. As the man began to head in that direction, Stellman shouted, "Hey!" and whistled to get his attention. He reached into his pocket and tossed him a small key ring with handcuff keys. "You'll need these to get him back to holding."

Then Stellman returned to the task of blotting his pants and fighting with the brown bits of paper towel that were now disintegrating all over his pants leg as he worked the stain from being bad to worse. "Ruined! Ruined! Of course. Why should I expect anything different?" After several fruitless attempts he was getting ready to go to the men's room, remove his pants and rinse the cuff in the sink when his cell phone rang. It was his boss.

"Hey, the escort is here for the prisoner. Where is he?" his boss asked.

"What do you mean, where is he? I told him what room he was in, how hard is it to find a freakin' room number down the hall?" He took in a breath and looked up to the ceiling in eye rolling disgust. "Hold on. I'll be right there." He hung up. "Damn moron dumbass." He slung the wet paper towels in the waste basket and exited the break room. Down the hall he met up with a different man than the one he'd almost collided with standing outside the door to room 402. He turned and looked up and down the hallway. "Where's the other guy you came with?" Stellman inquired.

"I didn't come with anyone," exclaimed the escort.

"I gave the keys to the other escort who was just here," he said with impatient irritation.

"*I'm* the escort," he said while he watched the expression on Stellman's face transform from irritation to total shock. Color drained from the interrogator's face. He lunged for the door to the interrogation room, bracing himself with one hand on each side of the door frame as he leaned forward looking inside the now empty room.

"Oh, no! No! No! Shit!" Stellman said while he turned to run to his boss's office. How the hell was he going to explain losing their prisoner!? Holy crap his ass was in a sling!

On the floor of the now empty interrogation room lay three AAA batteries and a plastic battery cover. But both the recording device and Marcus were gone!

CHAPTER TWO

As Marcus and his rescuer made their escape, Marcus had to be half dragged, and half walked by the man who struggled to lead him down the elevator to the bottom floor. They went toward a remote emergency exit at the rear of the building where Marcus had been interrogated. Numerous times Marcus's ankles would turn under, tripping him to the point of stumbling while his aid maintained a firm grip under one armpit for support. Nevertheless, he urged Marcus along quickly. Adrenaline, pared with the fact that he was taller and more muscular than Marcus helped him with the task of holding Marcus upright. They turned down a narrow hallway, but just before reaching the exit which led to a small parking area behind the building, it appeared Marcus had expended what little energy he had left in his traumatized body. He was visibly shutting down. He suddenly veered away from his supporter's grasp toward the wall next to them in an attempt to bring an end to their progress. He used the wall as sort of a vertical bed on which he so longed to be given rest. Marcus pressed his cheek against the cool wall and closed his eyes with relief. In exasperation, his rescuer tugged at his arm to no avail. He encouraged him to keep going saying, "Come on Marcus. We're going home. Hang with me buddy. Here," he said patting the left breast of his jacket. He reached into the inside breast pocket of his jacket. "Smell this," he said taking out an ampoule of smelling salts. He crushed it and held it to Marcus's nose. Marcus jolted from the smell and with a burst of anger furiously took a closer look at James for the first time.

"Counselor!" he exclaimed with unexpected recognition.

"Don't talk," he said leading him along again, "Just walk. I have a car waiting. Remember. Don't talk. Just rest, do what I say, and don't call me by any names at all," James instructed as he got Marcus back on track in their attempt to flee. James opened the heavy exit door leaving the mustiness of the old, dilapidated building behind them and headed for the car that had brought him there.

A cool blast of fresh fall air hit Marcus in his face upon leaving the building and it helped to revive him a tad more as they exited. This, plus the realization that he was actually being removed from captivity allowed him to muster just enough stamina to make his way the few final steps that were required of him. James raised his arm to flag down the silver Prius Uber car he had waiting for them. It pulled forward and without a word, the two men entered the back seat and the driver began to pull away.

"There's been a slight change," he said to the driver. "Go south one block and then turn left," James instructed.

The car started to make its way through a heavy flow of traffic while James took several nervous glances behind them to see if it appeared as though anyone was following them. He hadn't expected to have gotten Marcus out of the building as easily and quickly as he had. This was potentially just going to be a reconnaissance trip. In disbelief he marveled that it had been so easy to find and retrieve Marcus. He was sure mayhem would certainly break out at any moment. For now it appeared that they might actually have a chance at putting some distance between themselves and Marcus's captors, if their luck remained with them just a little while longer.

When the driver was finally able to make the left turn, James directed, "Now go three blocks and take a right, please." While traversing those blocks James handed Marcus a comb and quietly instructed him to tidy up his hair, which was still wet with a combination of sweat and grease from remaining unwashed for so long. Then he told him to tuck in his shirt to help erase some of the soiled, disheveled look of having been tortured for multiple days. Marcus silently did as commanded.

"Take another right and let us out at the building up on the left," he said, pointing in that direction. "It's the one with the lady out front wearing the orange jacket," he guided. "Right here. Yes, this one. That's great. Thanks."

As the car pulled over on the one way street, the men quickly exited the vehicle on the driver's side. Marcus followed James as he headed toward the door of the high rise office building. They went inside but immediately stopped and remained near the doorway they had just entered. "Keep your head low. Look down. Don't look up. We don't want any cameras getting a good visual on us," James said nervously keeping an eye on the Uber car while waiting for it to drive out of sight. James waited with Marcus a few moments longer before exiting out the same door they had just entered. Supporting Marcus by the elbow, they crossed the street and walked into a long shotgun lobby located in the building on the opposite side of the road from where the driver had just dropped them off.

Lisa Kirkman

Heads down, they made their way through the entire entry hall, past several banks of elevators, people and potted plants until they were able to exit on the next street just west of their initial drop point. Once outside on the sidewalk, James waved down a taxi and instructed the driver to go to Grand Central Station.

As they proceeded to their destination Marcus slept heavily as the taxi jostled his limp body like that of a rag doll. He was passed out in the seat next to James who took that moment to reach for his phone and text the following two words, "En route."

A reply came back immediately, "Already????"

Reflectively, James rested his left elbow on the window sill next to him and began to rub his temple in small, slow circles as his mind drifted over past and future events yet to materialize. He had not asked to be placed in the position of being the leader of eleven other people besides himself to where they were today. Here they were plotting the extraction of one of their members from captivity, for heaven sake. The liability was overwhelming him as he thought about the responsibility of protecting all his associates. Had he been wrong in his guidance all these years? Surely the events of today suggested that they had come to an apparent 'end of the road'. Was this the end to a task that had been centuries in the making. "What next?" he wondered. "What next?" This day had always been anticipated. But now what? The burden he was feeling weighed heavily upon him.

He remained this way in deepest thought until the taxi pulled into the line for arriving and departing passengers at Grand Central Station. James was then faced with the daunting task of awakening Marcus, who by this time, seemed absolutely comatose with sleep and was unresponsive to being shaken back to consciousness. Not wanting to bring any more harm to him than he'd already suffered at the hands of his interrogators, James resorted to pinching a pressure point on Marcus's shoulder to cause him some discomfort and was finally able to arouse him so they could exit the taxi.

As they made their way into the crowded station, Marcus looked to James questioningly to receive instructions regarding what their next move might be. James looked at the faces of those nearest them. As he sized them up he said in his mind, "Not Spanish, not Chinese, definitely not English"...then speaking in Hindi he asked those within ear shot, "Who here speaks Hindi?" When no one responded with a knowing glance, James proceeded to tell Marcus in Hindi that they had a plan to get back home. "Mara is here," he said. "She and Simon have cooked up a scheme to throw off any cameras that might be tracking us. So, when you see Mara, don't act like you recognize her. Simon....well.... you won't have to worry about Simon because you *won't* recognize him. He's got on a great disguise."

A short distance inside they came to a bench positioned directly across from the men's room. Sitting on the bench was a striking woman with an olive complexion. Her thick hair was slicked back in a shiny black bun. It was hard for Marcus to keep his eyes from darting her way because she looked so very different than he was used to seeing. It was normal for her to command attention simply because of what had become her biggest impediment. Her beauty was unforgettable. For someone who had to lead a life of being unnoticed, this Mediterranean goddess's beauty was next to impossible to disguise. However, for today she had been sent with Simon on this mission precisely because of her good looks. If she could cause a distraction away from what her comrades were executing, she would be an instrumental player in their overall plan.

Due to her disturbing past, Mara always dressed very modestly, but for today, she too was in costume along with Simon. Her costume was a pair of tight black jeans, knee high stiletto boots, and a tight black, scooped neck top that almost went off the shoulders. Her push up bra gave a hint of cleavage and Marcus fell victim briefly to the allure that she was meant to bring about.

Upon seeing Marcus and James, Mara stood and helped a rather portly, elderly man with wiry grey hair rise to his unsteady feet. He wobbled some as if starting to fall backward again onto the bench, but she caught him and steadied him before placing a walker squarely in front of him as throngs of people passed to and fro. She then gestured with a wave of her arm toward the direction to the men's room. The elderly man was actually their associate Simon who was in a disguise. He began to shuffle forward, leaning heavily upon the handles of his walker, taking steps that only inched along as he went. No one noticed this elderly man dressed in his long tan trench coat other than the occasional passerby who cursed him in their mind for being far too slow and distressfully in their way. Old people to them were just a nuisance that prevented them from dashing from point A to point B as efficiently as they had planned. Everyone seemed relieved when the old man finally got through the crowd of travelers and entered the men's restroom, leaving them to their fast paced, important lives.

James instructed Marcus to wait a moment longer as they pretended to read a schedule on the wall next to them while James kept a surreptitious eye on Simon's protracted progress through the wave of travelers. For a man who hated attention, it appeared that Simon was quite the drama king while in costume! James held back a laugh at the thought. Once Simon got inside the men's room, James told Marcus it was time for them to make their way in as well. They entered the opening to the bathroom which was a wide passageway with no doors. Directly inside that entrance was a privacy wall that the two men darted around in order to locate Simon.

◆◆◆

Twenty four hours later Marcus's interrogator had managed to piece together the Uber ride, surveillance footage at the two buildings and the taxi ride to Grand Central. James and Marcus could be seen on the Grand Central surveillance cameras going into the men's room, but there was no apparent evidence of the two ever coming back out.

CHAPTER THREE

Upon entering the men's room, James quickly directed Marcus into the oversized handicapped stall and slipped inside with him where they found Simon. He had already removed his trench coat and had hung it over one side of the stall while he continued to undress. His apparently stout physique was actually a soft sided briefcase and backpack filled with changes of clothing for James and Simon that had been hidden underneath his trench coat and strapped to his waist. Marcus was told to dress in Simon's disguise and once he'd done so, they topped his head off with the shaggy grey wig. Finally, when he was given Simon's walker, Marcus was actually grateful to have something to lean upon, given his still diminished state.

James and Simon redressed in all black like that of 90% of all the other New Yorker's in hopes of blending in as best as possible. James picked up the soft sided briefcase and Simon slung the backpack filled with their remaining clothing over one shoulder.

"Marcus, listen to me now. Here's the plan," Simon said in hushed tones putting his hand on Marcus's shoulder to get his full attention. He spoke almost as if Marcus was a child, not because he was being condescending, but because he knew that Marcus had been through some harsh treatment and was mentally compromised. "Mara will be on the phone with James. She's going to give us the cue when you should exit. We

MEETING AT MATTHEW STREET

want you to start heading out of the restroom at the exact moment we tell you to. Don't try to avoid *any* of the people who will be passing by. Remember, you're an elderly New Yorker on a walker. You expect everyone *else* to watch out for you and give *you* room. Got it?" Simon paused for a reply of acknowledgement. When one didn't come, he looked with worry toward James and asked with his eyes if he thought Marcus could pull this off.

"Marcus!" James reiterated, giving it his own try to convey the importance of their instructions, "You will walk out on cue shuffling along like Simon did when he came in here. We want you to walk out of here regardless of the number of people you might walk out in front of. Ok?" James hoped he'd get an adequate response out of Marcus. "Do you understand?"

"Yes. I'm supposed to walk out slowly on cue and piss off a bunch of busy New Yorkers," he replied. James cut his eyes over to Simon who smiled.

"That's our Marcus!" Simon said patting him on the back with satisfaction.

His accurate response was sufficient to convince Simon and James that he fully understood his role in the next move they were going to make in an attempt to cover their tracks before making their way home to the safe house. Regardless of his fatigue, Marcus was not unfamiliar with diversions and the art of disappearing in a crowd.

"It's show time!" Simon said, pointing his finger at James, directing him to proceed with the plan.

James phoned Mara who was waiting for his call on the bench just outside of the men's room. She answered, and leaned forward to see around a large trash receptacle sitting next to the bench. Once she had a better view of the interior of the station she began to keep James informed as she studied the crowd of people headed their way. A lull in people exiting the station meant that the timing was not right yet to send Marcus out, but when it appeared that a larger group was making its way toward the exit she began to instruct James saying, "Hold it.....hold it....almost there .....aaaand NOW!" She instructed.

"Go!" James told Marcus, and with great relief they saw Marcus push his walker straight out in front of a large group of travelers. The disruption caused some to stop abruptly in their tracks almost standing on their tip toes to keep from running into Marcus, while others shifted their paths to pass on either side of Marcus and his walker contraption. The confusion continued as those who were paying more attention to their cell phones than what was ahead of them ran into those who had stopped for Marcus. Others were looking toward Mara who was now standing and began to take her hair out of its bun, allowing the thick waves of silky tendrils to flow past her breasts on one side before she shook her head backward. She raised both arms and flicked the velvety river of locks so they cascaded down her back.

As Marcus inched further out, disgruntled people diverted their paths in such a way that some even maneuvered slightly inside the large open passageway to the men's room. As soon as that happened James intentionally dropped two file folders onto the floor so they would slide toward the edge of the exit. Simon and James both ducked down low to pick up one file each and using the cover of the divergent crowd managed to slip out of the men's room undetected by any cameras that might be trained on their location.

Simon pulled his black jacket collar up high around his chin and worked his way straight through the stream of people. He stopped briefly at a kiosk on the other side of the hall before heading back into the station.

James left the building and zig zagged out of sight on foot for several blocks while Marcus and Mara slowly exited the building and got into the car in which she had arrived. It was a car that had fake license plates on it.

Mara hoped to get Marcus back to the safe house as fast as possible, but not before taking a few random turns that took them through multiple neighborhoods and past run down businesses where it was more likely that they would not be detected by the ever present cameras of the day. Ring doorbells, and a plethora of other devices invaded the privacy of people who wished to remain unseen, unknown and undiscovered.

She made her final turn onto Matthew Street and pulled into the driveway of 2752, where a large green three story Victorian house stood centered upon a well-manicured lawn. Simultaneously, she pushed the button to the garage door opener. No one exited the car until the garage door was fully closed behind them.

Once inside the house, Libby, a woman in her late 50's who they all liked to refer to as "mom" met them immediately upon entering. Without a word she took Marcus by the elbow and led him to a small bedroom she had prepared for him on the bottom floor of the house.

She helped Marcus remove the disguise he was wearing as well as his shoes before helping him swing his legs up onto the twin bed she had turned down for him. She pulled down the shades that were framed by billowy folds of cream colored sheers, and turned off the bedside lamp before quietly leaving the room. She could already hear Marcus snoring by the time she gently shut the bedroom door and exited.

Libby returned to the kitchen where she found Mara. She had already changed out of her tight clothing and was now dressed in a baggy sweatshirt that hung low like a tunic well past her waist. She wore jeans and slipper booties that came up past her ankles. She was standing in front of the open refrigerator door looking for a jar filled with her favorite snack, Hearts of Palm. Mara found the container, placed it on the center island and removed a stick of palm. She wrapped it in a paper towel and began to peel the palm in long strips that looked like string cheese which she playfully dropped into her open mouth. Her part of the mission was complete and she was happy to be successfully home safe with Marcus back in the fold. She was also happy to have her stiletto boots off which she was unaccustomed to wearing. She had practiced wearing them for hours around the house to keep from looking like she had the legs of an invertebrate while playing her role in retrieving Marcus.

"So there's an emergency recall for everyone to come home?" she confirmed with Libby between bites of palm.

"Yes. Aaron and Peter are already here and are upstairs unpacking."

"Ahhh. The nerds are here," Mara noted.

"But they're such lovable nerds," Libby joked. "And, let's see...Amos told them at work that he had a family emergency and is en route," Libby said while removing some groceries from a bag sitting on the kitchen countertop. "He was a little upset about the recall because he was in the midst of preparing a special dinner for the First Lady. Some head of state visit I think. He was especially looking forward to it.... but now...." Her voice trailed off. She refilled a large bowl with fruit from a second grocery sack before placing it in the center of the kitchen island and adding, "Basically everyone else should be here in time for dinner, sooo if you'd like to be my sous-chef...?" Libby suggested hopefully while sliding a five pound bag of potatoes across the island toward Mara.

Mara pulled the sack closer to her and grabbed a knife out of the knife block. "Cooking for twelve. It'll be like Thanksgiving but without the thanks," Mara said with sarcasm and began to open the bag.

Lisa Kirkman

CHAPTER FOUR

Ron Evans sat in a darkened room on the 2nd floor of the unmarked building James had rescued Marcus from only days before. His desk was a long narrow ledge that spanned the entire length of one wall. Multiple computer monitors sat side by side across the expanse of the ledge. Each screen was filled with still shots or video footage set to loop repeatedly. He was so trained on watching the slow motion video obtained from Grand Central Station that he was unaware Marcus's interrogator, Robert Stellman, had entered his office and was standing behind him observing his progress.

As Stellman studied the many screens Ron was working from, he observed pairs of matched still shots. One photo would show a single person surrounded by a red oval outline as he entered the men's room. This subject was connected with a line to a second still shot of the same person encircled by another red oval showing him exiting the men's room. It became apparent that Ron was trying to find the two missing subjects, Marcus and his rescuer, through the process of elimination. By finding the footage of all the people who had entered the bathroom and exited again, he hoped to figure out the mystery of their disappearance. On the main computer screen he was playing the portion of footage where an old man on a walker was exiting as a crowd of people bustled past him. It was the only portion of footage he couldn't make heads or tails of.

MEETING AT MATTHEW STREET

Stellman leaned forward to get a closer look at the numerous still photos of Marcus's rescuer that were on one of the monitors when Ron realized Stellman was there.

"Any news for me?" Stellman asked Ron.

"Nothing!" Ron said in disgust. "I'm getting ready to start tallying people from some of the other video angles. One of the cameras that I really could have used was broken, so we've got nothing there. And this one.... ehhh, it's crap," he said pointing out the blurred lower corner and poor angle.

"They definitely went in there," Stellman said. "So keep up the hunt. Expand the timeframe. Expand the search perimeter, whatever it takes. By the way, I got word from the forensics team that there's no drop ceiling in the bathroom, so we know they didn't get out by going *up* and out." Stellman placed his left hand on the back of Ron's chair and leaned in for a closer look. Ron felt the heat from Stellman's body next to his along with a faint smell of cedar as Stellman asked what it was that Ron was looking for in the loop which was playing repeatedly on the main screen.

"Ehhh... it's just something that... I don't know. It's probably nothing, but," Ron pointed to a loop in play on the screen just to his right. "Over here, this is Marcus and your perp walking into the station. Watch Marcus's left foot... here!..and...riiiight there!" He tapped the screen. "See how his foot sort of points inward and he stumbles over his own toes?"

"Yeh. He was pretty fucked up when he left here," Stellman relayed.

"Ok. He also trips up once while crossing the street on that other loop," he said while pointing to yet another screen. "So...." he said, moving back to the main screen. "Take a look at the old guy coming in on his walker," Ron cued up a video of Simon shuffling into the men's room. "Look how his feet are pointed outward sort of splay toed. Right? Ok?...Now...." he toggled back to the loop he had been studying when Stellman first walked in. "You see this?" He said pointing to Marcus disguised as the old man exiting the men's room. "It's subtle, but right here, look.... toes not pointed out and THERE! Did you see it? A little bit of a trip over his left foot. I mean... it's nothing much but it's been bothering me."

Robert Stellman stood up straight and crossed his arms while taking a couple steps backward. With feet spread wide, back slightly arched, he shifted his weight from side to side while he thought. His eyes narrowed as he appeared to look at the space where the ceiling met the wall before reaching back over and tapping Ron on his shoulder to instruct him, "Add two more people to your team and concentrate on the movements of that old man." He turned and walked out. Things might be looking up!

MEETING AT MATTHEW STREET

CHAPTER FIVE

At 2752 Matthew Street it was decided that dinner would be served late so everyone could wait for David and Jerry to arrive from New Orleans before eating. They had started driving up the day before when James contacted them about the emergency recall. It was recommended that everyone drive instead of fly in case their identities had been compromised during Marcus's interrogation.

David was currently working as a pediatrics doctor at the New Orleans Children's Hospital. He was sharing an apartment with Jeremiah, who went by the name Jerry. Jerry was the on-site engineer for the hospital's addition of a $225 million expansion and renovation project. David was working closely with Jerry to design what he called the perfect surgery unit, a neonatal cardiac intensive care unit, as well as David's greatest passion, a new state-of-the-art cancer center.

David was all the children's favorite doctor at the center. He always had a stupid joke to tell and a gentle loving way. He knew special tricks for making painful procedures hurt less while making sides ache more from laughter. He knew when to be playful, but he also respected the wisdom of the children to be frank with them and talk seriously with them when discussing critical health matters.

There is no heart more open than that of a child and no mind more open to the future than the mind of a child who thinks they might not have a future due to cancer. David, or Dr. D as his young patients called him, had a mission to heal both the minds and souls of the children he was tasked with saving. Sadly, however, there were times when all attempts to cure had been exhausted without luck. When one of his precious patients came close to taking their final breath, David was known to make a visit to that child's room. He would then ask the family to please give him a quiet moment alone with his patient. Then Dr. D. would climb onto the bed and cuddle close, side by side to his young confidant. He'd reach into his white lab coat, remove a tiny book from his breast pocket and read seven amazing sentences to the child. Next, he'd whisper in their ear a question. "If I tell you a secret, can you keep it forever?"

Forever? This was often responded to with knowing eyes full of the wisdom and acceptance that forever might not be for very long. After agreeing with their favorite doctor to keep his secret, they would lend him an ear and listen intently as he whispered something so special that no one else could be trusted to hear it. Feeling his gentle breath against their ear tickled at first, but as he shared his secret with them, their beautiful big eyes widened even further and turned into eyes of awe and hope. "Please don't tell anyone what I just told you," David would plead concerning the secret. There was such sincerity in what he said that none of the children doubted what he had just told them was anything but genuine. No one thought it was cruel, or condescending, or a lie was being told to a dying child. These children were firmly convinced that what he had just told them was in fact quite real and not a joke at all. It was real! It was true! Many a child passed from this world to the next with less fear having agreed to keep Dr. D's sacred secret.

Unlike David's patients, his roommate Jerry liked working with burly adults. As an acclaimed engineer and contractor, he enjoyed the gruff characters who worked in construction. It was because they were "real" people, and not pretentious. Many of the contractors he dealt with were multimillionaires without all the airs often attached to people in "cleaner" jobs. Their cursing and profanity on the job was simply their unique form of expression, "color" Jerry called it. He was never offended by the things rattled off while these powerful men worked by the sweat of their brow and brawn of their limbs. They reminded him of his past. They were his heroes and all the men on his work crews could sense his admiration for their skill. He just wished there were more wanting to learn and perfect their skills in construction. He was witnessing craftsmanship vanish. Crews were shrinking by the day, as workers opted to stay at home and live off of government assistance, instead of having purpose and being able to admire the fruits of their labor. The only hope he could see for the future lay squarely in the hands of illegal aliens with whom he was able to communicate in Spanish and Portuguese when needed. Hard workers wanted to follow Jerry to whatever job he was managing. He just had to be careful to train a good replacement to leave behind. It needed to be someone his followers would attach their wholehearted loyalty to. Jerry knew that he had to reinvent himself before moving to a new location every twenty years, and it broke his heart to part company with his most promising apprentices. However, he surreptitiously followed their accomplishments with great pride after he moved on to a new project.

Lisa Kirkman

David had "his children" at the hospital, but Jerry had his "children." So what if they were hard as nails, covered in sweat and dirt with mouths that spewed profanities? These rough men were his progeny in whom he was well pleased.

As "his children," they could all tell you the message that Jerry continually shared with them. It was a message that sort of freaked some of them out because when he shared it, they honestly believed it. He would always take them aside, one by one and tell them, "God is watching you as you work. Believe me. Seriously. God is watching you and the work you do. And that is why you should always make sure it's something you'd want Him to see."

Thinking back to his words, many would have chills run down their spines remembering how he'd say it to them. It seemed like he knew what he was talking about from firsthand experience? Some of the more superstitious men on his crew actually quit because they thought he had "some weird juju goin' on"… That was their loss.

CHAPTER SIX

Aaron nimbly made his way down the three flights of stairs in the safe house at his normal quick pace from his bedroom on the top floor. As he neared the bottom floor, he could hear the sound of many voices coming from the large, but now crowded kitchen. Aaron always felt out of place in a crowd, so he slipped into the room while trying to remain unnoticed. He passed by his colleagues who all appeared to be conversing in pairs in order to hear one another better over the hubbub surrounding their unexpected reunion due to being recalled to their headquarters. As he passed each person, he was able to make out bits of the topics being discussed. In spite of wishing to remain unnoticed, as he worked his way through the crowd, he received a few pats on the back, a "hey buddy!" and a number of hearty handshakes as everyone greeted him.

James, who specialized in government intelligence was huddled with Phillip, who was in law enforcement. They were talking about people wearing masks at protests and that it should be outlawed. Simon, a researcher and writer, was talking to David about the latest archives to which he had recently been given permission to gain access. Peter, the group's tech guru was asking questions about the IRS programs being used at Andrew's office. Jerry, the construction engineer was talking to Mara about a mural he and David wanted her to paint in the new cancer center once it was closer to completion.

Lisa Kirkman

Aaron had scanned the room and made a beeline for Libby who was leaning against the kitchen sink by herself with a face absolutely aglow with satisfaction. She liked nothing more than to have everyone together under one roof. As Aaron approached her, she patted the countertop next to her as if to offer a place for him to join her, but first she reached over and cupped one side of his face with her right hand while firmly planting a big kiss on his opposite cheek. Aaron's self-consciousness faded. It was so reassuring to be loved like that. "Mom" was one of the few people in the world who shared physical touch with him and the warmth of her, both in body heat and affection, meant more to him than he could ever express.

With a bang the kitchen door to the garage burst open and Amos entered. He had to kick it open with one foot while balancing a large box in front of him. He said it was a surprise from the White House that he'd be sharing with everyone after dinner. He proceeded to press past everyone as they flattened their backs against the kitchen walls to allow Amos and *his box* enough room to pass by and exit the kitchen.

Libby placed a hand on Aaron's forearm and asked, "Aaron, hon, will you help Mara put out the food? We're ready to eat." Libby handed him two well-worn hot mitts. Then, waving a hand across the kitchen island in Mara and Jerry's direction she said, "Mara, excuse my interruption, but I think we should go ahead and set the food out." Mara went to the stovetop and grabbed two silicone pinch mitts so she could take the hot cornbread out of the oven.

Looking over Mara's shoulder as she passed him, Andrew exclaimed, "Oh yeh. Southern cookin'!"

MEETING AT MATTHEW STREET

It might appear odd that a group in New York would be setting out a spread of collard greens seasoned with smoked pork necks, cornbread, fresh green beans, squash cooked only in its natural juices, pressure cooker pot roast, and buttery mashed potatoes, but Libby was a collector of cooking styles from all over the world, and she knew this was everyone's favorite meal.

Her meals were always a surprise. One night might be Indian cuisine that would leave the house fragrant for days with the aromas of cumin, curry, cinnamon, cloves, garam masala, and cardamom pods. The next day might be a French reduction sauce over veal medallions on a bed of pasta al dente. Every meal was an experience and made with great care.

"That reminds me!" Jerry said. "Doc, where'd you put our little gift?"

David edged past the kitchen island and reached alongside the refrigerator where he picked up a mason jar wrapped completely in tin foil. It was unusual looking, to say the least, so he grabbed a kitchen towel, draped it over his left forearm and with the flare of a maître d' from one of the finest restaurants he handed the uniquely wrapped jar to Libby. "I dunno about the foil," he said. "Maybe it can't be exposed to the light or something, but one of my patient's fathers made this. It's a jar of Filé ... And judging by the size of the jar, it's a lifetime supply of the stuff," he laughed.

Libby took the aluminum foil-wrapped jar, held it appreciatively in her two hands and hugged it to her chest, taking special care not to drop the thoughtful gift that the two men had brought to her all the way from New Orleans. She unscrewed the lid and looked inside. The jar was filled with a fine green powder that smelled of spinach. She hugged David's neck and blew a kiss across the room to Jerry who let out a Cajun, "Ayeee," upon catching the imaginary kiss in midair.

"Good catch, bro!" Phillip congratulated him and gave him a high five and laughed.

In the dining room, Mara and Aaron smiled at hearing the comradery coming from the next room while they adjusted the two gravy boats, one on either end of the enormous table.

Mara hummed as they worked. She was always singing. In fact, when she went to sleep at night she would have psalms from her youth, hymns from the past 300 years or contemporary Christian tunes playing in her mind. When she would awaken in the middle of the night, she would discover that her mind had switched from one sacred tune to another. Apparently, no matter what she was doing, her subconscious was always singing to God. Suddenly, Mara's tune turned from humming to words and she finished the tune she was singing with a playful, overdramatized flare. While holding two serving spoons in her fists she brought both of her hands toward her heart and began singing to Aaron, "For I am Yours, and You are mine," she sang as she swept her hands toward Aaron in a grand flourish and then brought them back to her breast. She ended her playful serenade with a laugh and dove the serving spoons into two bowls on the table.

She didn't know that what she had just done sent butterflies dancing within Aaron's heart toward her. He wished her words were truly being directed toward him. His heart ached knowing it was not, in fact, the case.

The table was nearly set. They always ate family style with large pots placed on trivets all down the center of the table. Libby collected trivets like she did cooking styles. There were metal trivets, woven grass ones from Africa, intricately carved wooden trivets with inlay of Mother of Pearl from India, and crocheted ones that Mara had handmade with love for Libby.

Taking one of Mara's crocheted trivets, Aaron sort of fanned it in the air before putting it down and shyly said to Mara, "I was admiring your latest art projects upstairs."

Other than Aaron's bedroom on the 3rd floor, Mara used the other side of that level for her art studio. Large canvases on multiple easels were scattered here and there in various stages of completion. As she felt inspiration strike, she'd work on one and then another, always waiting for "the spirit to move her."

"I always marvel at your ability to use light in your oil paintings. It's…it's absolutely breathtaking. I don't know how you do it," he said nervously. He admired her many talents and she intimidated him with her skill as well as her beauty.

"Thanks," she said. "But I feel like I'm in a dry spell right now. I'm just not *feeling* it. Ya' know? And I *hate* not having a project to be totally immersed in at all times. It makes me feel worthless if I'm not busy."

"It'll come," he encouraged. "The best results come when you let ideas simmer for a while."

"Good things come to those who wait? Huh? You know, James told me that Abraham Lincoln said that better things come to those who hustle," Mara teased while making a final inspection of the table settings from one end to the other before proclaiming approvingly to Aaron, "Looks good to me." Then she shouted over her shoulder toward the kitchen, "Dinner!!!"

Everyone began to file into the dining room where they took a place standing behind a chair. Seats had never been assigned, but it was a tradition that everyone sat in the same place when they ate together. Libby was at the head of one end of the table and James was at the other end. To Libby's right was Aaron and to her left was Mara. Marcus's seat remained empty while he continued to rest.

When Libby pulled her chair out, Aaron habitually placed himself behind her to help her slide into place while everyone else took their seats.

"Simon, will you say the prayer, please?" Libby requested.

In Hebrew, Simon began, "Blessed are You, Lord our God, King of the universe. Bless the food we are about to eat and the hands that have prepared it. May all that we do be pleasing in Your sight. Amen."

"Amen," the rest of the table repeated.

Other than this formality, the rest of the meal was quite noisy and informal as the food began to be passed around the table.

The events from earlier that day were not brought up and remained awkwardly absent from the discussions that were taking place over dinner. Until they could speak with Marcus, there was little to be shared. All that was known was, Peter was sent to pick Marcus up at LaGuardia Airport and was surprised to see him being escorted out of the airport by a police officer and two men in dark suits and sunglasses.

When Peter saw this, he followed them and was able to keep enough distance from them throughout the airport until he observed the men in suits pushing Marcus into what appeared to be a Government issued, black SUV.

MEETING AT MATTHEW STREET

They were parked in the no loading zone outside the airport terminal and no taxis were immediately within sight. Peter's car was in short term parking, so he couldn't follow them any further.

In exacerbation, Peter hurried to the baggage claim area and offered to pay a Marine who had come in on Marcus's flight to get Marcus's bag off the carousel for him. Peter claimed he was suffering from a bad back and needed help. He wanted to see if the bag might offer some clues about the abduction, but he also didn't want the abandoned bag to be used by a surveillance team to track anyone claiming it later and following them back to their safe house.

The Marine was happy to help, wouldn't take any pay, and brought the bag to Peter who was waiting for him. He had huddled next to a large pillar by the exit, trying to remain as much out of sight as possible. Peter quickly removed Marcus's luggage tag and airline barcode tags. Now the plain black bag looked virtually indistinguishable from all the other black bags in the crowded airport. As Peter reappeared from behind the large column, he looked like most of the other travelers hurrying along with a cell phone pressed to his ear. He had James on the phone with him. The pursuit to find Marcus and his whereabouts had begun.

Over the days that followed, Peter, who was versed in computer hacking, and James, who had special clearance through his work in government intelligence; ran into multiple, confusing dead ends. Whoever took Marcus was CIA-like, Interpol-like, but apparently an offshoot of both. They were either deep state, or some sort of covert public/private entity.

Lisa Kirkman

When James and Peter finally ran down the location where they thought Marcus had been taken, it was discovered he was being held in an old, unmarked building with no affiliation to any of the agencies that they were more familiar with. When James walked into the building to find Marcus, he was astounded to see that there were no metal detectors, no security guards, no passes required for the elevators. Nothing. It was a covert operation using "plain sight" as their disguise.

MEETING AT MATTHEW STREET

CHAPTER SEVEN

When the meal was finished, the men took turns clearing the table and cleaning up while Libby and Mara set up the Chabudai, a long low table they had acquired in Japan which was located in "the meeting room." Distributed across the top of the table were an assortment of desserts that were popular in various parts of the world. There was cheese and jellied fruit called Goiabada from Brazil for those who liked a more sweet and savory combination. Marcus's favorite Eclairs were present in his honor. Several slices of a firm New York Cheesecake were flanked by small bowls filled with various toppings. Next to the table on the floor, sat Amos's mystery box that he had brought to them from his job at the White House, where he worked as the head chef.

When things had been cleaned up sufficiently, everyone trickled into the meeting room, a large long room which ended in a beautiful, Victorian cast iron fireplace.

The room could be described in only one word. Eclectic! This was a room meant for comfort and the only way to make twelve people of diverse tastes and backgrounds feel comfortable was to give each of them their own spaces.

That meant there were twelve mismatched chairs in a wide array of colors, patterns and styles as well as twelve works of art behind each chair. Several exquisite Persian rugs dotted the hard wood floor. The only common denominator that the room donned were matching side tables to the right of each person's chair. The lone exception was Aaron's. Since he was left handed, his side table sat to the left of his chair.

Atop each table was a lamp of that person's choice and on a shelf underneath the side tables were any number of personal items including books in different languages, artifacts from various time periods, or boxes filled with knick-knacks.

The only area that was different from the others was Mara's which was located in the front right corner next to the doorway. As an accomplished pianist, she also had a baby grand Steinway piano behind her sitting area. Instead of one work of art, she displayed several of her oil paintings on the wall space around the piano. Her paintings were changed out frequently as buyers acquired her masterpieces.

Mara entered their meeting room alongside David and immediately did a happy jump and skip before squealing, "Looky, looky," while playfully tugging David over to her area of the room. She then changed her tone as she waved Vanna White beauty hands toward her newly acquired chair saying in an alluring voice, "It's a Human Touch Zero Gravity massage chair!" She patted the arm of the chair and removed the controls from its side pocket, "I'll even let you take it for a test ride."

"It looks a little like an electric chair to me," David said, poking at the cream colored leather before sitting down on it. "What does it do?"

With excitement, Mara turned the chair onto its demo massage mode, and then retreated for the duration of the demo to sit in the doctor's chair, a vintage, brown leather cigar club chair with small crazed lines that ran all over its worn leather surface. David called them laugh lines.

Libby took a seat in a Queen Anne winged chair with carved walnut legs from the 1700's. Jerry took his place in a huge, overstuffed La-Z-Boy recliner, and before Amos took a seat in his mid-century modern Barcelona chair he called for everyone's attention.

Amos knelt down on one knee and opened the brown cardboard box he had come in with. From within, he extracted twelve glorious, 14k gold leafed boxes. Each box had the White House seal in cloisonné on the top and when opened, revealed a set of four tiny petit fours exquisitely decorated with the most perfect, microscopic details. When the First Lady was asked if she wanted real gold added to the iced details, she refused the offer, saying that gold should be admired by the eye and not consumed by the mouth because the eye was more discerning.

Amos began to pass the boxes around explaining, "Our pastry chef made these and the First Lady was gracious enough to send them when she heard of my 'family emergency'," he said using his fingers as quotation marks before leaving the last box next to Marcus's chair.

Astounded by the box's beauty, Peter exclaimed, "Imagine what these could be sold for on eBay!" Everyone looked around the room at one another in agreement with Peter's assessment of their potential value.

With that, Libby added, "Anyone who would like to donate their empty box to the warehouse fund can leave it with me before my next run to the unit." Libby was house mother, historian and warehouse manager. As a collective, they had always pooled their resources and stored valuables in a warehouse until they could be sold in times of need or held until an item could appreciate in value and be sold at a tidy profit. These funds would be used to support the various causes they came across.

As everyone marveled over the ornate boxes and sampled some of the delicious confections inside, Marcus entered the room and surprised everyone with his presence. They figured he'd not be seen until the next day! Deep hollows shown beneath his eyes and he was in need of a hot shower. Nevertheless, his arrival to the meeting room meant that they could now find out what had happened to Marcus and discover if his captors had successfully coerced him into revealing the group's most sacred secret.

Libby did what any mom would do. She jumped up and ran to the kitchen to fix a plate of food for Marcus while David rose from Mara's massage chair and offered it to Marcus. He declined the offer and proceeded to his own Eastlake platform rocking chair near the fireplace and gingerly took a seat. He was still quite sore from being cuffed for days to a hard, unpadded chair.

Libby handed him a heaping plate that he took several bites from before setting it down on the side table next to him. He knew why everyone was there. They'd been recalled on his account and were awaiting an explanation.

"Tell us what happened," James eagerly inquired for the group while shifting to the edge of his seat, elbows on his knees so he might get the best view of Marcus from where he was sitting.

MEETING AT MATTHEW STREET

"Well…. You tell me!" he said bewildered. "The plane had just landed, I'm just sitting there and the captain says that there would be a slight delay in deplaning. I'm like, not concerned. I'm thinking, Peter is here to pick me up and will wait for whatever the heck is going on, so I see these two guys and a policeman come on board. I'm just checkin' it all out and was *totally* not expecting them to stop next to my seat and ask me to leave with them." He looked back at James, shrugged his shoulders and shook his head in disbelief.

James frowned and asked, "What were you doing before coming back to the states?"

"I went by my office in Hong Kong to…"

"Hong Kong!? We have a mandate to avoid China. Facial recognition cameras are everywhere Marcus! Seriously? Hong Kong? What were you thinking?" James chastised.

"I wanted to close things down before returning to the states. I had some artifacts and gold in my safe there. You know"…he shrugged ashamedly, "and they'd make for a nice contribution to our account, so I figured I'd be OK if I did a quick in and quick out."

"That was a risk that shouldn't have been taken," James said shaking his head.

"Could you tell what agency picked you up?" Peter asked.

"No. I kept looking for some sort of identification, but never saw any badges, paperwork, forms….nothing. I'd say it was covert. Nothing was done by the book. They kept asking where I was from and I'm pretty sure I told them…" he looked at all their faces trained on him and then added, "I think I told them everything."

The room erupted in moans, worried looks and disgruntled grumblings.

"There's something else," he added and the room came to an abrupt hush. "Early on there was an older man who came in by himself. It was weird. He just stood there for a long time sort of sizing me up and then he said, 'I know you're one of the twelve.' That's all he said. Then he laughed at me, and he left."

"What did he look like?" asked James.

"Really old... Short... Late 80's maybe. Covered in age spots all over his face. I mean, covered. Bags under his eyes. His mouth was turned down on the sides and his lips were all wet and reminded me of liver. The bottom lip was sort of narrow in the middle and plumper on each side and he talked with his lower lip poked out. There was something about his wet lips that... I don't know, they grossed me out. So I looked down to keep from looking at his lips and I saw that he had on something like surgical shoes or...I don't think they were Birkenstocks. Some sort of overly wide shoes. All I can remember was thinking that he was scary for an old man. Not weak looking, but really...spooky?" he said grasping for a description. "That's all I can say to describe him. It wasn't just his appearance, but an entire vibe that I got off of him," he paused in reflection. "I'd have to say that the entire experience was unremarkable, except for him."

Who were these people? What did they know about them? A pall fell over the group as everyone considered the implications of Marcus's unexpected news.

What Marcus didn't recall was that his own facial expression of shock upon hearing the man suggestion that he was one of twelve gave the old man the precise answer he was seeking. There was no question in his mind that he had just located one of the twelve people he'd been looking for over the past few decades. No question at all!

The older man who creeped Marcus out was Viktor Hoven. He had been using state of the art computer programs which were running photos of people's faces that had been taken as far back as World War II. These programs were cataloging the images for him using the finest facial recognition programs that China had to offer. He knew that what you couldn't find out about a person from social media pages like Facebook, you could discover on your own by using Chinese facial recognition technology. Knowing a person's associates could help you flush out spies within your own organizations. There was no denying that. But since his youth Viktor's mentor had warned him specifically of twelve people who had been placed on earth to disrupt his progress. But now with technology working for him even while he slept, his goal was to find and eliminate these twelve people before they could stop his twisted mission to disrupt nations and crash economies.

So far, he had been successful at collecting photos of at least five people who kept appearing on the fringes of photos. They were never seen in the forefront. Never in the limelight. Often seen in audiences at dedications, ribbon cuttings or award ceremonies and these same five people might appear in a 2004 photo looking the same as they did in a 1954 photo taken 50 years earlier.

As these computer programs provided more information about the twelve individuals he was searching for, the knowledge of their existence excited him.

Knowledge. Hoven's mind turned to Daniel 12:4 which spoke of the end times and of a world where "many would dash about and knowledge would increase." Lovers of knowledge, he laughed to himself. Lovers of their precious *smart* phones, he scoffed, patting at the phone in his breast pocket. Oh, how he was loving today's knowledge. Technology was indeed the tool he needed to help him increase his own power!

MEETING AT MATTHEW STREET

CHAPTER EIGHT

Upon hearing the words that the old man said to Marcus, Simon felt ill. He cut his eyes to James who was looking his way, clearly making the same connection that he was. Simon's mind went back to the summer of 1930 when he had heard that phrase "one of twelve" used once before. He had been part of a tour group visiting the Vatican where he was hoping to find a way to gain access over time to the massive library that the Vatican had collected and housed. As a writer, he knew there were manuscripts there that were of great interest to him, so one of the first steps he took toward obtaining access was to visit the site as a simple tourist before attempting a more serious approach.

Falling back from the group he tried repeatedly to engage members of the tour staff in conversations and was finally successful in detaining one such person while the group moved into another area with the main guide. During the side conversation he had struck up with the guide, a commotion materialized down the hallway they had just passed through. Suddenly a woman's screams could be heard as she cried out in blood curdling cries for help that echoed throughout the massive halls. The sound of her running feet could be heard coming closer until finally a young woman, in the later stage of pregnancy came barreling around the corner. Grasping the entryway with superhuman strength she flung her swollen body through the archway and into the alcove where Simon and the guide stood, dumfounded by her appearance. She lost her footing as she rounded the corner and fell with the sound of flesh squealing across the marble floor.

Before Simon could go to her aid, a team of priests rushed in behind her. Upon seeing them, the Vatican staff member gripped Simon's arm in fear, digging his fingernails deep into his forearm. The staff member recognized who these priests were and what they were known for.

The woman began to growl at the priests with an inhuman sound that made the hair on Simon's body tingle and stand on end.

"I'm sorry you had to see this," the staff member said taking a few steps backward in fear. "She must have escaped from an exorcism."

Five priests attempted to bring her under their control, but she fought them off fiercely, sending one crashing into a nearby wall knocking the breath out of him. Then she backhanded another who fell unconscious to the floor, his cheekbone shattered. More priests arrived and joined in until she was surrounded. Like a captive animal she crouched and rocked from side to side on her wide spread feet as she looked for a possible escape. Suddenly, seeing her chance, she ran through a small gap between two of the men and defying the laws of gravity and human ability she ran up the side of one wall to a height of about 9 feet before coming back down outside of the ring of men who had previously been surrounding her. Before she could leave the alcove, however, the group threw their bodies on top of her, bringing her to the ground. They dragged her briefly by her arms while her legs flailed violently leaving black heel marks across the floor in stark contrast to the white marble tiles. But, when they stopped to lift her onto her feet, her attention turned toward Simon. Her face then contorted into that of a gargoyle and she hissed at him. "What are you looking at?" she asked Simon before spitting a huge wad of green phlegm at him. When Simon looked down at the mass that landed near his feet, he noticed that it began to undulate as if it were alive. Maggots writhed within the slime. Seeing Simon's reaction, the woman let out a cackling, mocking laugh. As they continued to lead her away, she strained to look behind her at Simon and in a demonic voice she shouted back toward him, "You've met your match one of twelve!" Simon could hear her laughing well into the distance.

The staff member standing beside him appeared ashen faced and a cold bead of sweat ran down his face. He took a handkerchief out of his pocket and with shaking hands he dabbed at his brow. Assuming that the prophetic message had been aimed toward him, the guide immediately abandoned his post and never returned to his Vatican job again.

Simon had only mentioned his disturbing encounter to James who suggested that it not be shared with the others.

♦♦♦

Later that same August night in 1930 at 3:15 A.M., a man dressed in a Cardinal's robe stood hidden in the shadows near one of the gated entrances to Vatican City. He muttered impatiently. He was supposed to have been met at 3 A.M. but his collaborator was late! He was risking being discovered by the Swiss Guard if he waited much longer.

More time passed before he was finally able to make out the glint of a car with no headlights on coming down the alley toward where he was hiding. A Fiat 521 Weymann-Sedan pulled up with a driver in the front and the dark, unidentifiable shadow of a man sitting in the back.

The driver stopped the car and stepped up to the far corner of the gate. From the shadows, the Cardinal stepped forward. He was holding a sack in one hand. Without a word, the driver handed a leather coin purse through the bars of the gate to the Cardinal who placed the pouch within the folds of his robe. Then the Cardinal lifted the sack to chest height and carefully maneuvered the cinched bag through the bars, guiding its contents along the way. Once the bag had successfully made it beyond the Vatican walls, the driver turned on a sharp heel and presented it to the shadow figure in the back seat. As the drawstring end of the bag passed over the threshold of the car window, tiny white shriveled fingers of a newborn baby breached the cinched top and grasped at the edge of the opening. A bony hand from within the car gestured for the driver to come closer. He leaned in to receive a message from the figure inside.

The driver returned to the gate and said he had a message for the Cardinal, "I was told to tell you that you've been a good and faithful servant." The driver returned to the car and as the back window raised, the Cardinal heard the muffled sound of a baby crying before the car engine started and it disappeared from sight.

MEETING AT MATTHEW STREET

The Cardinal reached into his robe and extracted the pouch, heavy with gold. Looking at it in the moonlight he noticed that his fingernails were still stained with blood from the afterbirth. He would have to wash them *again*! He felt a small twinge of melancholy and sighed. He had always hoped to hear the proclamation that he had been "a good and faithful servant…" he just hadn't expected it to come from the man in the shadows. Looking skyward, he caught sight of the clock tower looming above him. The time read 3:33. He knew it was God's subtle sign to him that God was aware he had just aided the devil and therefore mocked His Holy Trinity. The Cardinal placed the pouch back into his robe and smiled. He was important. It didn't matter to whom.

CHAPTER NINE

Having heard what little information Marcus could share about his abduction, James stood up and proceeded toward the fireplace where a large book sat atop an ornate book stand. The stand was considered to be the group's most precious treasure. It had been hand crafted by two generations of artisans. The father taught his son, and the son improved upon the father's skills in the making of this exquisite piece. Everyone agreed that if they were ever faced with fleeing due to fire or other catastrophe, this would be the one item that they would save. The book stand looked like a narrow lectern with high relief wood carvings on the main shaft of the stand which depicted the twelve Disciples of Christ ascending up the shaft as if climbing a fig tree. Near the top of the stand was St. John, the disciple described in the Bible as the one who Jesus loved, reaching toward Jesus while offering him a fig in his outstretched hand. And at the very top of the shaft was the carving of Jesus with his arms raised in support of the platform upon which sat a large family Bible with gilded edges.

This artifact was from the Cologne Cathedral where in 1797 the cathedral was occupied by French Revolutionary troops and the prisoners of war who were being held there. When the prisoners began to use the nave's finely crafted wood furnishings for firewood, this stand had been saved from its fiery fate by the man tasked with cooking for the prisoners. Because of the depiction of the 12 Disciples of Christ, the book stand had become a symbol of their own twelve lives.

James placed his hand on top of the open page of the Bible wishing that wisdom could be absorbed through his hand and that he'd know how to properly lead the 11 people sitting before him who were hoping desperately for his guidance. He looked at the words on the page, words that had been largely ignored and disputed over the past 2000 years. He began reading the Holy Bible aloud starting at Matthew 27:50 which recounted the death of Jesus on the cross.

"Then Jesus shouted out again, and he released his spirit. At that moment the curtain in the sanctuary of the Temple was torn in two, from top to bottom. The earth shook, rocks split apart." He looked up at their faces. Some were nodding with recollection.

At Matthew 27:52 he continued, "and tombs opened."

"Yes!" shouted Libby.

"The bodies of many godly men and women who had died were raised from the dead. They left the cemetery after Jesus's resurrection, went into the holy city of Jerusalem, and appeared to many people.

The Roman officer and the other soldiers at the crucifixion were terrified by the earthquake and all that had happened. They said, 'This man truly was the Son of God!' "

"Amen," said Libby, while a tear ran down Mara's cheek.

James finished reading from the Bible and looked upon the faces of the very same people that he had just read about. Tombs had opened and *these* godly men and women were raised from death.

Several eyes turned to David who appeared to be transported in thought through time. His hand was over his heart. His fingers lightly tapped upon his chest with a double beat and pause, double beat and pause, like a heartbeat. He had been the only one of the twelve who had been given permission to reveal his identity under certain circumstances. As a doctor who dealt with many terminally ill patients, either through his work with Samaritan's Purse and Ebola patients, or now with children battling the final stages of cancer, he had been given the approval to tell the story of their death and resurrection to give hope to those who thought they were hopeless. First he'd read the passage from the Bible to them and then tell them, "I've been where you are. I died. It's NOT final. Believe me. Don't be afraid!"

David had met in counsel several times with fellow physician, Luke, where they discussed Jesus's words in Luke 18:27. Jesus encouraged mortal men by saying that the things that are not possible for humans to do are indeed possible for God. David knew this. The people sitting in that room with him *knew* this!

The room remained quiet for a moment before Libby solemnly spoke, "Let's let Marcus eat his meal and tomorrow we'll have fresh minds to think about what all of this means." She stood up and got Marcus's plate and led him to the dining room.

Everyone filed out and James joined Marcus in the dining room where the two spoke further about his experience.

Libby returned to the meeting room and watched James with great admiration as he sat in the next room with Marcus. James had been a member of the city council in his first life. He was known to be fair and just. He had been chosen to be on the council because of his wisdom and ability to make all who came before him feel that whatever the determination, no matter on whose side a decision fell, everyone felt that the results were justified. He had been offered bribes that could have helped his family greatly, but he always refused them and trusted in God.

After being raised and becoming a member of the twelve elect, James often took jobs with the government in whatever country the group happened to settle. He would take a position as an advisor or interpreter to higher level officials. As an interpreter, he often was privy to information that only the highest officials were made aware of. This could be a precarious job, even at his lower level status. There had been times when the government he was working for was overthrown by a coup and the officials he worked for were imprisoned or slaughtered to make way for a new government takeover. He was at risk of being killed during such takeovers. In Ethiopia, even the musicians who entertained the administration were imprisoned.

While some members of their group promoted positive causes, it was decided it was equally essential for other members to work against negative influences. So James was tasked with encouraging leaders to make good and just decisions.

Libby reflected back with pride to one of James's greatest moments while working in that capacity. It was during the American Civil War.

James had walked across the West Yard from the War Department to the White House. Upon entering he passed large throngs of people on the First Floor who were waiting for the open "Public Hours" to begin so they might bring their petitions and pleas directly to President Lincoln. The White House in those days was open to anyone who wanted to enter during the twice weekly sessions and the crowds were sometimes impassable with many toting weapons of their invention which they wished to pitch to the government for purchase.

President Lincoln noted, "For myself, I feel—though the tax on my time is heavy—that no hours of my day are better employed than those which thus bring me again within the direct contact and atmosphere of the average of our whole people. I call these receptions my *'public opinion baths,'* and their effect upon me is both renovating and invigorating."

James ascended the stairs to the second floor corner office. In a leather satchel under his arm he carried a letter from Charles-Louis Napoleon Bonaparte addressed to President Lincoln. James had just completed the translation of the letter and upon seeing the empty room, he placed the satchel where President Lincoln could read the correspondence at his convenience.

As he turned to exit, however, he was startled to see the President on his knees in the opposite corner of the room.

"Oh! Pardon my intrusion, Mr. President," he said. "I was unaware of your presence." Seeing the president on the floor, James became concerned and queried, "Are you well, sir?" As the president made an effort to rise, James approached and took him by the arm to help the president to his feet.

"I am as well as possible, I surmise. You discovered me not fallen by illness, but driven to my knees by overwhelming conviction that I had nowhere else to go," he said motioning toward the floor. "I fear my own wisdom is insufficient and I turned to divine intervention in my time of need," the President explained.

"My apologies for interrupting your private time with the Creator," James said.

"Alas, the Creator was not available," Lincoln said with a heavy heart. "I was praying for a 'public hour' with our Lord, but it appears He is not as accommodating as I."

James knew from previous conversations that President Lincoln struggled at times with his faith and was eager to assist if possible.

Lincoln continued on, "Nearly all men can stand adversity, but if you want to test a man's character, give him power!" he bemoaned.

"May I inquire as to the source of your angst?" James ventured.

"I am to determine the fate of the Confederate soldiers and their leaders at the war's conclusion. Many are demanding of me a most harsh punishment of these men. As I turned to God's word, admittedly in folly, I opened the Bible and with eyes fully closed I asked God to guide me to His message. Alas, my extended digit," he said while holding up the index finger of his right hand, "fell upon the verse Matthew 5:5, a beatitude stating that the meek shall inherit the earth. My dear James, I'm afraid meekness is the opposite of what my advisors wish of me at this juncture," he said deflated.

"With all due respect, Mr. President," James offered, "I would like to tender my linguistic assistance regarding that verse, if you are so inclined." James paused and

Lisa Kirkman

President Lincoln motioned with his hand to proceed. "I would submit that I am rather dismayed over its translation. Based upon my interpretation you may, in fact, surmise that God did indeed use this verse to speak His divine will upon you."

"Proceed James, please." President Lincoln took a seat and motioned for James to join him by taking a seat next to him.

"Sir, I have come to understand that there are some words that are unique to their original language and in this case the word our King James Bible uses here is 'meek'. Blessed are the meek: for they shall inherit the earth," he turned to the President who shook his head in agreement. "But sir, the original word in Greek was praus. Praus was a military word that related to horse training. You see, Mr. President, the Greek army would find the wildest horses in the mountains and gather them to be broken. After extensive training they separated the horses by category. Some were of no use at all, while others were broken and could then be used for bearing burdens. A few were useful for ordinary duty, but sir, only the finest of all could be elevated to the status of becoming a war horse. When a horse passed the ultimate conditioning required to be deemed a war horse, its state was then described as being *praus*. Praus, sir, is meek? Hardly!"

President Lincoln moved from a position of sitting with his arms crossed in front of him to leaning forward with his hands on his long and lanky knees in order to take in James's words as if ready to pounce should a single word escape past him.

James continued, "So you see, a war horse had power under authority, and strength under control. It had learned to bring its wild nature under discipline and control. It would respond to the slightest touch, stand firm in the face of heavy cannon fire, thunder bravely into battle, and yet stop at the mere whisper of its rider. That is the definition of our King James word 'meek.' "

President Lincoln got up and walked toward the window overlooking the unfinished Washington Monument and stood with his hands clasped behind his back in contemplation.

Gently James concluded, "Blessed are those who have weapons but keep them sheathed. Do you see why God may in fact be speaking to you through verse Matthew 5:5? If you show mercy to our Confederate brothers, would that not be a praus act on your part?"

James quietly left President Lincoln to his thoughts, but the following day he found a hand written note from the President on his desk in the War Department. The poor penmanship was unmistakably that of the President's. It read in large bold letters: **I am Praus!**

Below that the President added, "Thank you, James, for helping God's word speak to me."

When the Civil War ended it was resolved and extended "unconditionally, and without reservation a full pardon and amnesty" to the Confederate soldiers and it was ordered that they return to their families, in a gracious act of "sheathing the sword." That wasn't meekness. That was the greatest display of strength the United States had ever witnessed.

Because of his wisdom, James was asked to be the leader of the group of twelve. But at this moment, that was a designation he would gladly like to delegate to someone else.

Lisa Kirkman

Now that the meeting room was empty, Libby stepped up to the open Bible and turned to another page and reread Luke 9:27 while thinking back to her first life.

She had been resurrected as a 58 year old. Although everyone rose with perfectly healthy bodies, they maintained the appearance of the age that they had been when they passed away. At 58, her age was on the upper end of the normal life expectancy for the time period of 33 AD during her first life.

Before her death, Libby had lived in Bethsaida and was an outstanding woman. She epitomized the perfect wife mentioned in Proverbs 31. She was up early providing for her family, handled the family's finances well, worked with her hands to keep her family well clothed, and she always tended to the poor people of her community.

On one occasion, shortly before her demise, a friend asked her assistance while she hosted a man who was being referred to as a prophet. He and his followers were going to be visiting the friend's house and because she was going to be preparing food for so many people, the hostess asked if Libby would come over and help by pouring beverages and serving the guest's needs.

As one of her duties that evening, Libby took a wineskin and poured a portion of its contents into a jar and then added a set quantity of water to the wine to soften the flavor of it, as was the practice at that time.

She then set about serving the beverage to the guests.

As she entered into the room where the visitors were all crowded, she observed that everyone was quite intent upon listening to the one gentleman who was speaking. They were literally leaning toward him to take in every word he spoke.

MEETING AT MATTHEW STREET

Libby poured two glasses before reaching the speaker's cup. She felt embarrassed that she might distract from his narrative by serving him, so she timidly reached for his cup and poured it while turning her back away from the group. But as she placed it down again in front of him he said, "I tell you the truth." Then he reached out and grasped her by her outstretched wrist as he finished the statement, "Some people who are standing here will not die before they see the kingdom of God." * As the crowd murmured with excitement over this proclamation, he looked into Libby's eyes and said, "Thank you. You are a pleasure in God's eyes."

Libby remained transfixed for a moment. She didn't like compliments. She felt unworthy of them. But in this case, she wasn't sure why, she felt as though this man was not offering false flattery, but was conveying a genuine love and approval toward her. It went beyond appreciation of her simply serving glasses of wine to the group.

She spent the rest of the evening listening intently to the words of this man named Jesus.

*Footnote: Matthew 16:28, Mark 9:1, Luke 9:27

Lisa Kirkman

CHAPTER TEN

Over the millenniums scholars have been disturbed by the verse, Matthew 27:52. Many wanted to prove through earlier manuscripts that this verse had not existed and had been added at a later date, proving it inaccurate. But that verse had always been present, even in the earliest known writings ever found. Nevertheless, some argued that it seemed "out of place" and not in a proper order sequentially.

What they didn't know was that it *was* sort of an added passage that the original writer, St. Matthew, had not recorded in his first draft. But after having a dream where an angel instructed him not to forget to mention those who had risen from their tombs, Matthew added a brief statement about them. It was brief because he was instructed to keep the twelve who had risen safe from being discovered until they were called to come forward by God to fight the evil one.

The twelve original Disciples of Christ already had targets on their backs after Jesus's crucifixion. Paul was beheaded, two died by crucifixion, one by burning, another by stoning and there were various other brutal means by which Jesus's disciples died. Only John appears to have lived until he succumbed to old age. The risen twelve were meant to carry on in anonymity, which perhaps was the first diversion tactic they learned as a group. Anonymity meant they should promote a message and not themselves, always working in the background to see that seeds were planted for others to cultivate.

On the day that the tombs broke open, 12,000 Godly people rose from their graves and roamed all over the region from the Jordan to the mountains for forty days.

Even though the Bible didn't give the event much notice, there were other accounts of the momentous supernatural occurrence that were recorded by the Romans. They were known for their excellent record keeping and in the Vatican Archives, a letter was found taken from "Acta Pilati" that mentioned the miracle. It was a letter penned by Pontius Pilot, written to his emperor, Tiberius Caesar which read:

To Tiberius Caesar, Emperor of Rome. Noble Sovereign, Greeting: The events of the last few days in my province have been of such a character that I will give the details in full as they occurred.

(The guard) said that about the beginning of the fourth watch they saw a soft and beautiful light over the sepulcher. He at first thought that the women had come to embalm the body of Jesus, as was their custom, but he could not see how they could have gotten through the guards. While these thoughts were passing through his mind, behold, the whole place was lighted up, and there seemed to be crowds of the dead in their grave clothes. All seemed to be shouting and filled with ecstasy, while all around and above was the most beautiful music he had ever heard; and the whole air seemed to be voices praising God.

On the day Jesus ascended into heaven 40 days after his resurrection, all the risen souls came down from

Lisa Kirkman

Mount Amalech to join him and ascend with Jesus. That is, all except for the twelve elect who when they didn't ascend with the others felt exceptionally vulnerable and confused.

"Why weren't we taken up with the others?"

Imagine for a moment you are in a civic center, it seats 10,000 people and it's filled to capacity. Next, imagine an additional 2000 people standing in the center, on the open floor below you. Finally, imagine in your mind's eye all the souls disappearing in an instant. Suddenly, there's a deafening silence. Only twelve people remain, scattered throughout the massive expanse of space, looking bewildered. You look around and see an individual perhaps way across the arena on the far side. Only two are left on the previously packed floor, turning in circles, searching for more faces. You see another person 20 rows below where you are standing as you continue to survey the entire scene unfolding before your startled eyes.

If the twelve remaining individuals had been dumbfounded to be raised from the dead, you'll now have an idea of just how astounded they were to find for whatever reason, they were left behind!

MEETING AT MATTHEW STREET

CHAPTER ELEVEN

Robert Stellman diligently continued his investigation into the missing men who had alluded him so easily. His career was on the line to find them, not only with his direct boss, but also because he had been greatly surprised when he was informed that the elderly head of their organization, Viktor Hoven, had made a special appearance to meet briefly with Marcus while he was being held for interrogation. It had been at Mr. Hoven's bequest that Marcus be apprehended upon arriving in the United States to begin with.

Surveillance cameras in Hong Kong had provided Mr. Hoven with positive facial ID of Marcus. The Chinese were always happy to help Hoven when he needed a small favor. A small favor meant only a million dollar bribe that Hoven had to hand over.

It was just another day at the office for Hoven to obtain U. S. secrets for a million dollars and then sell them to the Chinese for four million dollars.

"Why did every politician in the U.S. want a million dollars to commit a crime?" he often wondered. It was so unoriginal.

Bigger international favors might cost a few billion, but that didn't faze Hoven. It was just the difference between a few extra zeros on the end of a series of numbers. That, and how many pockets he'd have to line along the way. Bribery was so simple. He wondered why more people didn't get into his line of work?

Lisa Kirkman

Currently, Hoven squarely had ten heads of state helping him with his goals to disrupt society. Divide and conquer, yes, but then destroy it! That was his motto and his mission. Happy people are content. Angry people cause instability. Instability allowed Hoven to step in and take charge. "Never let a good crisis go to waste?" Who needed to wait for a crisis to happen when you could create your own?

He and his six sons were instrumental throughout the world in crashing economies while profiting from their destruction. Occasionally, a president or Prime Minister might come along who would not side with him. That wouldn't matter much. The leader before would have been so cooperative that they would have imbedded so many minions within the country's top departments, that Hoven's plans would still be executed. A temporary change in leadership only meant that the minions had more work to do surreptitiously keeping his finely tuned machines running behind the scenes. Another election that Hoven funded for his handpicked candidates would put things right again. In fact, Hoven sort of enjoyed those temporary lapses. It allowed him to see just how powerful he had become. Running a large country, without the head of state knowing they were actually only a figurehead being played like a puppet, thrilled Hoven to no end.

Hoven felt the countries he controlled were like musical instruments in a symphony orchestra. He was a masterful maestro standing ready to manipulate them as he saw fit. With a wave of his baton he would transfer $33 billion dollars from one country to another who would then disseminate the funds to sympathizers running for offices, or paying off bribes that had been promised.

MEETING AT MATTHEW STREET

Some funds were placed in hidden bank accounts, while others simply wanted to keep theirs in an underground bunker. Of course, money always went to the news outlets who would report only the news Hoven allowed them to release. Raising his hands in a grand crescendo he would transfer deuterium oxide to a dictator who needed the heavy water to progress with their creation of a nuclear reactor. And for the grand finale? Oh! This was just the overture. In his mind he heard the cacophony of his future grand finale ringing throughout the entire world: Trumpets blaring, cymbals clashing, kettle drums banging, gongs crashing, great dissonances, bombs bursting, and uproarious discordance. He took in a deep breath and felt alive with excitement.

Stellman had heard many stories of Hoven, but he only knew the basic, general information that most people knew. Things like, he was very well funded, always got what he wanted, and had huge international connections. Some people referred to Hoven as being a philanthropist that organized major, yet sometimes controversial causes. He was also deeply involved in the politics of several countries.

That part surprised Stellman more than anything else. Normally, a person concentrated his efforts around the country where they held citizenship. But for some reason Hoven seemed to want to be everywhere at once.

Stellman hadn't a clue what Hoven wanted with Marcus, but he planned to find out as he entered Ron Evans's office and once more found him hunched over screens full of video footage. "Hey Ron, how's it coming? They said you wanted to see me?"

Ron pushed off with his feet, thrusting his chair so that it rolled backward a few feet across his office floor before he threw his arms up into the air in disgust. Shaking his head he said, "I followed one fella who I'm pretty sure was the man who walked off with our guy from here. He did this zigzag thing on foot for a few blocks, in and out of buildings and stuff before I lost him. But here," he walked his chair forward and pointed to two screens, "I was able to track the old man on the walker in the car that he and the woman left in."

Stellman got excited and bent closer to get a better look.

"But here's where I lost them. They leave a populated area with businesses and go into an older neighborhood where the trail goes dry. But look at this," he said pointing to the third screen over, "Here you see them pull into a McDonald's just before I can't track them any longer. They've already passed a ton of other McDonald's along the way, so the question is, why *this* one?" he said tapping the screen while looking up at Stellman.

"Because… they've been to it before and it's close to home?" Stellman surmised.

"Maybe. Anyway, it's all I've got. Sorry, man. Wish I could be more help, but…." Ron shrugged.

"How 'bout get me the address for that McDonald's and tell me what post office services that area," Stellman requested, "and give me a good print out with a photo of the car, the girl and a good one of Marcus if you can."

With a few clicks of his mouse, Ron had the photos printing out on a machine on the other side of his office. He slipped them into a large manila envelope before handing them over to Stellman.

His only hope was that the post office he was about to visit might turn out to be a small hub verses a larger distribution site and that someone there knew his escaped perps.

Stellman took the elevator to the 4th floor and told his boss he would probably be leaving soon to check out a lead. As soon as he walked out of the office his cell phone chimed with a text message. Ron had texted him the post office address that serviced the area near the McDonald's.

Once he'd gotten into his car, Stellman took his phone out and called his girlfriend. They had been dating for almost a year and he was getting serious about their relationship. But if this investigation didn't pan out, he thought it might be possible he'd be fired. He didn't want to make any major commitment to marriage if he'd be unemployed soon.

His friends wondered why a guy who had dated a ton of women over the years, would even consider something like marriage when he had the freedom to see whoever he wanted whenever he wanted. But this time it was different. This woman was different.

"Hey babe. I'm not going to make it for lunch. I'm following a lead on my missing guy. Wish me luck because it's not looking too good," he said.

Stellman's girlfriend offered him words of encouragement, but they fell flat on Stellman's ear because he knew that what he was about to pursue was a huge long shot. Nevertheless, he appreciated having a sympathetic friend to share his concerns with. He had never had a girlfriend in the past that he felt like he could confide in. So this was very unique and a first for him.

Forty five minutes later Stellman pulled up to the post office address Ron had sent him. He felt a twinge of hope when he saw how small it was. "This just might work," he thought.

Lisa Kirkman

Stepping into the post office he passed a row of post office boxes to his right before coming to the counter straight ahead of him. Posted all along the edge of the counter were hand written signs. "No cell phone use while at the counter," "No credit cards," "Closed from 11:30-12:30."

Stellman stepped up to the counter and waited. No one showed as he looked for a bell or some means of getting attention. Finally he yelled out, "Hello?"

From a side room a man in his late 20's with shoulder length hair emerged. The way he walked to the counter area made Stellman have expectations of being addressed with a "Hey Dude" greeting. Instead the man simply apologized and said he didn't hear him come in.

Stellman proceeded to reveal his official business with the man, hoping this guy might be impressed with what he was about to share.

Dramatically looking over his shoulder, as if to insure privacy, Stellman leaned over the tall counter and proceeded in a guarded voice. "Hello. I'm Agent Stellman, and I'm in the midst of an investigation of a fugitive who might be somewhere in this area," he said with his most official voice possible.

The young man's jaw dropped and eyes opened wide as his thoughts turned immediately to terrorism. "Am I like in danger or anything? Is this guy armed?"

"No, you're fine, but you would certainly be doing a service to your country if you could take a look at these photos and let me know if you've seen this car," he said while whipping the photos out of the envelope with a little bit of an impressive flourish, "or," he said tapping on the images of Marcus and Mara, "either of these two people."

MEETING AT MATTHEW STREET

The young man bent over the countertop to get a good, close look at all three images set before him but Stellman could tell by the shaking of the clerk's head that there was no apparent sign of recognition.

Seeing this, Stellman suggested, "Are there any mailmen who you could show these to, to see if they've seen these people?"

"I don't recognize any of them, but yeah, if I can hold onto these photos I'll share them with the other people who work here later today when they come in from their routes."

"Great! I'd really appreciate it. The guy I'm looking for speaks a couple different languages, so if you see any overseas letters or anything like that, it might be a clue to his whereabouts."

"Oh! Well that wouldn't be on one of the routes. That would be that large postal drawer over there," he said pointing, "that gets all kinds of weird mail. Stuff addressed to lots of different people with really awesome stamps from all over the world. Lots of those flimsy envelopes with the stripes and stuff. Yeah. Absolutely, it's that one over there."

Stellman looked over his shoulder at the bank of boxes. "Which one?" he asked.

"F-11 on the bottom row about halfway down."

"Who comes in for the mail from it?" Stellman asked.

"Uhhh…. A lady comes in, all covered in something like a Muslim thing on her head."

Stellman thought back to the unusual language Marcus first spoke to him in and said, "Yeah. Uh huh. That could be right… and how often does she come in here?"

"I'd say it's not a set day or time, but maybe once a week?"

"Man, I really appreciate it," Stellman said offering his hand to shake that of a fellow patriot, "I thank you and your country thanks you," he said patronizingly while gathering up the photos.

What he was thinking, however, was "You just saved me from having to obtain a warrant and get this info legally, you idiot."

"I'll be hanging out here for a few days. I'd appreciate it if you wouldn't tell anyone why I'm here. If anyone asks, tell them I'm a postal inspector or something like that," Stellman requested.

He left the post office and went two blocks to a gas station where he bought chips, crackers, a Snickers candy bar and a 32 oz. drink. He would need something to get him through his stake out while he waited outside of the post office for the next week.

MEETING AT MATTHEW STREET

CHAPTER TWELVE

Days had passed since Marcus's return and everyone's recall to the safe house. Meetings were being held regularly at 2752 Matthew Street. The discussions were often heated, because a consensus was trying to be arrived at concerning their future as a group. Until they could agree as a whole about what they would do from this moment on, they would not stop having these discussions.

A few minutes before the appointed time they had set for the next round of talks, Libby walked into the meeting room and found Aaron standing in front of Mara's chair. In his hands he held a blanket that Mara used when she was cold. He had it clutched to his face breathing in the scent of her perfume.

Libby approached him and rubbed his back gently. She knew his feelings toward Mara and when his eyes met hers, he felt comfort in knowing that someone else could empathize with the anguish he was feeling. They were discussing disbanding; and avoiding ever seeing one another again for the rest of whatever amount of time God had put them back on earth. It was a scary time. These were the only people he could call family.

From the beginning, they had decided that in their resurrected state they would never marry. Obviously, they couldn't marry someone who would see that they did not age, and for the sake of unity, they decided that they could not marry either of the two women in their group either. Furthermore, they had a mission to serve others and to deny themselves of their own pleasures. They were influencers sent by God to carry on as Jesus's behind the scenes disciples.

To deny themselves of *any* contact with one another by disbanding? Please! This just couldn't be the direction that they would agree to, hoped Libby.

Aaron inhaled one last time before neatly folding the blanket and draping it over the back of Mara's chair. The fragrance she always wore was called Angel. Such an appropriate name considering Mara's history with their group.

To Aaron, he thought that her beauty would probably rival that of the angels, but she also sang like an angel. He would often linger in his 3rd floor bedroom to hear her singing while she worked on her paintings. But it was in 1971 that she was first, literally mistaken as an actual angel.

In 1922 in Bengal, Mara was working there as a missionary and befriended a bright-eyed 12 year old girl named Agnes who loved hearing all of Mara's stories of the mission work she had done. Agnes would beg her unmercifully for more and more stories until Mara would finally acquiesce. Mara assumed correctly that this child would never make the connection that Mara's apparent age would make the wide range of her experiences virtually impossible. A normal person could not have accomplished as many good works as Mara had accomplished. But Agnes never figured that out.

When Mara's time to move on had come, the group had a rule, they never stayed in one place longer than twenty years at a time. Then, they would have to relocate to an area so different from where they had been that the possibility of being recognized and dealing with the same circle of people would be as remote as where they had moved to.

This method of relocating was easy at first. Five hundred miles from Jerusalem was a great distance for people who traveled on foot. Over time the distances that were required for them to make meant relocating to different countries, which then escalated to moving to different continents in order to avoid recognition.

But in this modern era of travel, the world seemed to have become too small for them. Air travel made it easy for a person to be in Africa on one day and the United States, the next. Knowing this, they began to rotate their members in and out of service. This gave them an appropriate break between the hands-on works that they loved doing most, and allowed for an absence from face to face involvement.

This necessity first became most apparent to them in 1967 when Mara was working with orphaned children in Nepal. One young girl there had come from a family that had been marked for murder by a warring faction and Mara knew that the only way to keep the child safe was to transfer her to a more remote orphanage where she could not be found. David told her of an orphanage being run by the Missionaries of Charity in Calcutta. He had visited them while issuing inoculations in the area and he spoke very highly of their work.

So, Mara set out with her young charge and delivered her to the orphanage in Calcutta. As she knelt down to say her goodbyes to the little girl, the head of the facility, a

Lisa Kirkman

50 year old nun, caught sight of Mara from the other side of their compound and in amazement she called out to her, "Mara?"

Mara looked up and recognized the person coming toward her. She was aware of who this was, but was confused because they had never met before.

The nun approached Mara and grasped her hands in her own and gazed into Mara's familiar eyes. However, in her mind she was busy calculating the time since they had seen one another last. Mara would have been in her mid-20's in 1922, but that would make her 70 now!

Confused, she asked, "Were you a missionary in Bengal?"

Mara felt her heart leap and denied ever having been to Bengal, but the nun saw the expression on Mara's face and was certain she had struck a nerve. This was very curious, indeed!

Mara quickly made excuses about having to go and hastily left the orphanage, leaving the nun confused by what had just transpired.

It wasn't until 1971, when Mara read a book about one great Christian's life that she was able to connect the dots. She realized that a pre-teen named Agnes with whom she had shared her stories, had taken the seed she had planted about missionary work, and become one of Mara's most fruitful protégés. In 1931 when Agnes took vows of poverty, chastity, and obedience to become a nun, Agnes changed her name and from then on was better known to the world as Mother Teresa.

Twelve years after Mara had first been recognized by Mother Teresa in Calcutta, Mother Teresa was awarded the Nobel Peace Prize in 1979. Being of small stature, she could barely see over the podium from which she addressed the audience. But there, in the midst of the crowd she *thought* she caught sight of Mara. Mara was so happy for Mother Teresa that she had to take the risk and attend the ceremony.

Taking the award in her frail but productive hands Mother Teresa looked out into the crowd and saw Mara, appearing just as she had 57 years earlier, peeking out from behind a man in the audience that she was trying to hide behind. That was when Mother Teresa felt in her heart that Mara was an angel, sent from God to watch over her and guide her along her path of humble service.

She was then asked by the presenter, "What can we do to promote world peace?"

Turning to the person who had asked the question, she replied, "Go home and love your family." But when she looked back out into the audience to seek Mara's approval over her response, she discovered that Mara had disappeared.

Mara had ducked out, feeling her heart swell knowing that she had touched an amazing life, and that she was not an angel, but someone who had fulfilled a small portion of what God had brought her back to accomplish for Him. She was an influencer.

CHAPTER THIRTEEN

Mara came into the meeting room after Aaron and Libby and sat down at her piano and played while the others filed in. Some entered the room already arguing over their concerns. Mara tried to lose herself in the music by playing louder to drown them out until the meeting was called to order. She didn't like the conflict this was causing.

"If we disband, we will increase our odds of escaping notice," said Amos.

"I work in intel, give me a chance to find out who is looking for us," said James.

"I'm good with our staying together and working behind the scenes. How many online charities do we have so far, Marcus?" asked Simon.

"We have sixteen strong ones. I'm sure we could add more," said Marcus.

"I'm good with that," offered Peter. "We'd all pitch in to manage the sites and the inquiries and just work from the safe house."

"Forever from the safe house?" asked Phillip.

"I've recently been dealing with a woman who's been working from her home for the past 30 years," David submitted.

"What does she do?" Marcus asked.

"She's making all the printed giveaways that we're getting for when we have the hospital grand opening. Pens, cups, shirts…our marketing director calls it swag."

MEETING AT MATTHEW STREET

"How's working at home going for her?" Marcus asked.

"Ehhh. She said she feels socially out of touch and worries that she doesn't fit in like she used to when she worked in an office with other people. But, I gotta tell you, regardless of what we decide, I'm not leaving the hospital until the project is complete. And when it's done, I'm sticking around until I see that it's running smoothly," said David.

"Yeah, I'm staying put with David," said Jerry. "The build needs to be completed. It's one of our greater works in recent years that we've helped make possible. We've got to see it through."

"Can you believe that they're *still* after me for a billboard photo?" David said to the group. "I keep telling them I don't *do* photos but the CEO actually threatened my job the other day if I didn't participate in the photo session."

"That's the problem! There's no privacy!" said Phillip. "Everywhere you turn you're on a camera, or someone wants to take your photo and post it on their Facebook page without your permission. It's awful!"

"Oh! That reminds me. Mom," said Amos, "when you go to our P.O. Box, be on the lookout for some F-dot bills for me."

"What's an F-dot?" Libby asked.

"Florida Department of Transportation. I was taking the Suncoast Parkway out of Tampa and they have a couple of toll areas where they snap a photo of your car as you go under a bank of cameras and then mail a bill for the toll amount. Anyway, they're legit and need to be paid."

Lisa Kirkman

"Do you hear what we're all saying?" asked Andrew. "Staying the way we've been will be impossible! For heaven's sake, I have retina recognition at work now and they've had my fingerprints on file at the IRS for years! Staying anonymous is impossible!" Andrew said about his work at the IRS.

Everyone in the group had jobs that could help them meld into society while continuing their mission to promote good or to diminish evil, whether it was a job to assist in obtaining fake Social Security numbers, a computer hacker to create fake identities, government intelligence workers on the inside, working at the White House for far reaching connections, law enforcement, or managing the finances for the many philanthropic works that they were promoting and managing. They were a symbiotic unit and what was being proposed by some of the group was to break up into twelve separate entities, effectively divorcing themselves from one another. But no one could quite figure how they could survive in this new climate of technology without one another's help.

"What if we move?" suggested James.

"No!" Libby agonized, putting both hands over her mouth. She had petitioned in the 1920's to be allowed to run a household from one location for longer than twenty years at a time and Jerry built her the house of her dreams here at 2752 Matthew Street. She had been so careful to remain unnoticed. She shopped at remote locations, always rotating them so she wouldn't be recognized, and now, with on-line ordering she could finally see that deliveries to their doorstep could allow her to exercise yet another option for keeping the house supplied to her liking without being discovered as "the lady who never ages."

MEETING AT MATTHEW STREET

"We could shut down and do nothing for twenty years," suggested Simon.

"That's easy for you to say, Simon. You're a writer. You use whatever pseudonym you want for each book you write and just keep on doing your thing! How can you just kick the rest of us into oblivion?" Peter accused.

"Are you saying our missionary work isn't important?" Marcus asked Simon.

"How much and how long is enough?" asked Simon.

"This is getting out of hand," said Libby.

"I've sacrificed my happiness to keep you guys running around with ID's and passports all these years," Andrew complained.

"This is getting out of hand," Libby repeated.

"We're all pitching in as best we can, *Andrew*. Don't think that I enjoy the stress of what I do for heaven's sake!" said Phillip raising his voice.

"This is getting out of hand!" shouted Libby. "Stop it, please!"

"This is seriously messed up," Jerry said. "I'm questioning this whole darn thing," shaking his head while losing hope for a resolution.

"Really Jerry?... Simon? Are all of you suggesting that the purpose of our resurrection is complete? It's over? We're done?" Libby queried, knowing the answer as the room fell quiet.

Breaking the silence, Mara kidded, "I don't know about *you* guys, but I was resurrected with the most *awesome* complexion," she said hoping to soften the mood.

Jerry rubbed the two day's growth of beard stubble on his chin and said in his gruff voice, "Personally, I didn't notice an improvement with *my* skin."

"My skin was great!" Aaron added resolutely.

"You had *leprosy* Aaron! Of course your skin would be better!" Mara jabbed.

Aaron's face broke out in a red blush unlike anything they had ever seen.

"You had leprosy?" David asked. "You're kidding me! How did I go two thousand years and not know that?"

Libby reached over and patted Aaron on his knee consoling him. She had known about this as the group's historian. She knew about all of them, but she was unaware that Mara knew Aaron's secret.

The scars of leprosy in Aaron's psyche were deep. Mental scars, not physical. He had had to yell out "unclean" everywhere he went before his resurrection. People ran from him and he had to beg for scraps of food that were thrown at him out of fear of getting too close to him. Libby knew that Aaron had always struggled with the baggage of his first life.

"How did *you* know, Mara?" David pressed.

Now Mara felt ashamed for having exposed Aaron's secret. She lowered her head and looked into her lap with shame. "My dad told me to avoid him."

The room fell silent. Tears welled up in several pairs of eyes, Andrew struggled to swallow as a lump caught in his throat as their lives before resurrection came back to slap all of them fully in the face. After all, they had all suffered and died. They saw death regularly during their first life. The average life expectancy was only 40 years in the first century.

David painfully remembered the deaths of three of his children who all died before the age of four. Infant mortality was so very high. And his wife died in childbirth. He felt ashamed for having made such a big deal out of hearing the news about Aaron. From the standpoint of a doctor, he tried to justify it in his mind, it was just curiosity on his part to find out more. With today's medicines it was curable. But he should have respected the feelings of someone who had suffered greatly in his past and he knew better. He regretted his words.

Words can hurt and some words can convey more than others. Over time as the twelve traversed the world they came across words that they "collected," so to speak. They were often words that were unique to a specific language. For instance, in Brazil there was a word, saudades (sou doj ez), which the group particularly liked. It had no suitable English translation. The closest word in English might be a homesickness. But saudade was more of a nostalgic or melancholic longing, or yearning, or a sense of loneliness and incompleteness. No matter what language they were speaking in at any given time, the group would use this Portuguese word because it was a perfect word that came closest to their feelings when separated from one another.

Another word that meant a lot to them was their mission word. The group chose the Greek word splagchnizomai (splag-nē'-zo-mah) as their mission guide. The Bible states that Jesus had a "splagchnizomai," a stomach turning, gut wrenching empathy for those who were hungry. As a group, they decided that their splagchnizomai, or stomach turning empathy was for innocent people who were faced with abuse. With that in mind, the group always focused their efforts to help the innocent; abused children, orphans, people placed in slavery, and those forced into the sex trade.

Now, as they faced the possibility of abandoning their united splagchnizomai for helping the hurting people of the world, the group discovered they were already feeling a sense of saudade at the thought of separating from one another.

With heavy hearts, the meeting was adjourned.

MEETING AT MATTHEW STREET

CHAPTER FOURTEEN

As the elect filed out of the room Aaron went straight to his bedroom upstairs and closed his door. The anguish of finding out all these years that Mara had known him as someone her father had instructed her to avoid was one of the heaviest feelings of grief he'd ever felt. He had centuries of experiences to compare this moment to and this was by far the lowest he could remember ever feeling since his painful pre-resurrection years.

A few minutes passed when he heard a gentle knocking at his door and Mara's soft voice on the other side asking to speak to him. "Aaron. I'm sorry."

He didn't answer because he was too bitter to respond, and after a bit he heard her leave. He just wanted to be left alone in his misery. He was still unclean. Still an outcast after two thousand years. How could God bring him back to this world but not eradicate the memory of his pain, or the humiliation that he still found himself brooding over?

Aaron had lived in Mara's community and worked some as a teacher before contracting leprosy from a visiting uncle. He led a short, painful, miserable life of being shunned everywhere he went. Because of his compassion for people who were different from others, he had always taught school since his resurrection and worked primarily with the handicapped. He loved them all dearly.

Lisa Kirkman

Most recently, he had started to work with inner city children from broken homes. These youth were being wooed by drug dealers and gang leaders to reject the society which had rejected them and turn to a life of crime. Despite his efforts, many saw the glitz and glamor of what was being offered to them by the dealers as being far more interesting than the straight path Aaron was recommending. But out of every one hundred he worked with, if only one succeeded in life, and carried his message along, then he would use that life as reassurance that he was going where God wanted him to be as an influencer.

Downstairs the atmosphere was heavy. Amos got up and went into the kitchen to start making the evening meal. He had given Libby the night off from her normal chores of cooking their meals.

"What's for dinner?" Jerry asked as he passed through the kitchen.

"Duck a l'orange," Amos replied while skillfully maneuvering throughout the kitchen. The normal gaiety that this announcement would have provoked from the group was not present today. Instead, their minds were wrestling more with the question, "How many more meals will we be able to share together as a group from this day forward?"

Jerry proceeded to step outside to get some air and then decided to make his way to the workshop he had built for them behind their house. Once inside he'd see if there were any projects on his workbench that Libby had left for him. Every time he returned to the safe house she managed to put him to work with a list of "honey do" repairs because he was her Mr. Fixit. Plus, Jerry felt that the only way to kill time was to work it to death.

MEETING AT MATTHEW STREET

In the kitchen, David poured a glass of wine for himself and one for Amos before he began to help him with the meal prep.

A bottle of wine, David thought while moving the bottle to the side. A sense of gratitude swept over him. He didn't grow the grapes, press them, ferment them or bottle the end product. It was amazing how far they had come over the years. It still struck him that he could buy anything he wanted and that it was possible with such little effort on his part.

The heavy atmosphere in the safe house and everyone's anxiety made David reflect on a time in England just before the year 1000 when meal prep was possible only after months of working the land. Those were back breaking days! The yield was dependent upon the weather and pests, but as if that wasn't enough to deal with, there were times when they had to hide the activity of threshing the grain they had harvested. It was normally done on a hilltop where the wind would separate the grain from the chaff, but if the marauding Vikings saw the process as it was taking place, they'd come running to take their meager harvest away from them after all the work had been completed. So devastating. Yet so easy now, he thought, to open a bottle, a can or a freezer filled to capacity. He had tremendous respect for today's farmers who continued to deal with weather conditions that might ruin their crops and their livelihood.

His appreciation for their struggles to survive over the centuries contributed greatly to the heartbreak he and Jerry felt for the hurting people of third world countries where they normally worked to bring them help and hope. Their feeling of empathy was deep because they had been there. They had lived it.

Meanwhile, Libby remained in the meeting room alone after everyone had left. She looked around the room and studied every detail of it, committing it to memory while thinking of what it would mean if they were forced to leave.

When she took in a deep breath, her lungs stuttered as if she had been crying. Then, she slowly got down on her knees and began to extract a stack of bound books from under her side table. Each volume covered highlights of the life of one of the twelve elect. Some of the pages' edges were brittle even though they had been copied and recopied again and again over the centuries. First in Hebrew on papyrus, later on leather parchment and more recently on a variety of paper products, with her most current accounts written in English.

Recently, she had asked Peter to computerize them and hand them over to Simon to maintain in a digital format. But Libby liked her tangible volumes and ran a loving hand over the top book to brush away any dust that had settled there. These were her children, she thought, hugging the stack close to her breast. This was her family now. This was her purpose in life to take care of these eleven souls that had been placed in her care by the one true God, Yahweh, Jehovah, Adonai.

"Father, please don't separate us," she prayed.

Sitting down in her Queen Anne Chair, she opened the first volume. The book's spine crackled slightly as the book opened across her lap and she began to reflect over and read each of their names, scanning her notes about each of their amazing lives.

Simon had been a Rabi, or teacher of the Jewish law. Because he was an intellectual, educated and adept at doing research, his job after resurrection was to study, teach and write.

As a writer he was able to work under numerous pseudonyms over the centuries. He had published translations of the Bible in multiple languages, he'd written commentaries, published sermons, and wrote numerous books on finding one's purpose as a Christian. With the Bible being the most published book in history, the accumulation of all of Simon's various works throughout time would surely come in as a solid second. He was the only one in the group who was able to maintain this work regardless of where they moved.

Simon believed in a saying attributed to Mahatma Gandhi, but dated back even further. "Live like you'll die tomorrow, learn like you'll live forever." And since he didn't know God's ultimate plan for him, he did just that.

Libby was Simon's proofreader. She knew that he was a kind soul who took her criticisms very well. She loved his works and found him to be quite eloquent. His translations had brought the word of God to many nations who would not have gotten it otherwise.

She opened the next volume.

Peter had been a boat builder. But he was quite astute at studying design, as well as the dynamics of propulsion, drag, and stability. He dedicated his life to not settling for the status quo, but to the study of improvement. He always thought that there could be a better way of doing things and he followed all the latest cutting edge technologies.

For this reason, Peter was tasked with seeing that the group advanced through the ages as the world advanced. It meant going from horses to cars, cars to planes, and letters to emails. He needed to acquire the modern tools necessary to train the others in their group in the most efficient means of funding their philanthropic projects. This meant handling their finances, as well as his most recent endeavor, learning about and managing their electronic presence with webpages featuring their top projects throughout the world.

Libby knew that Peter had patience and self-control because he had taught her how to use the internet. Even though she did so kicking and screaming, she was indebted to him for having shown her what she needed to know, with one exception. She was certain that Facebook was the sign of the beast and she refused to have anything to do with it. Period!

As she lifted Peter's volume from her lap, a photo of a young Billy Graham fell out from its pages. She picked it up and smiled.

Peter often became involved with an organization to see how it worked before recommending it to their group for funding. It was during one of his examinations that he met the then 29 year old Billy Graham in early 1948 while helping him with an event in Augusta.

Billy Graham had been hired by Youth for Christ as a full-time evangelist and Peter was a volunteer who would travel with them to each location where they held a rally. He helped with renting a field or parking lot where a tent could be pitched. Once set up, Billy Graham and his friend Charles Templeton would hold a crusade or tent meeting where they'd take turns preaching the gospel and asking people to accept Christ as their savior.

On this occasion, Peter was under the tent, that had just been erected, and he was putting chairs out in rows

MEETING AT MATTHEW STREET

when Billy came in. Billy stepped onto the platform where he'd be preaching later that night and decided to rearrange the chairs on the riser to his liking. He was going to sit while his friend and roommate for the night, Charles Templeton, presented his portion of the message. Billy positioned his chair, and then walked up the aisle a few rows to see how it looked, before returning to move the chair a little more to the right on the platform. As Billy was doing this, Charles Templeton entered the tent and started looking around for a misplaced box of Bible study booklets to be handed out at the end of the evening, after the invitation was given. When new believers came forward to profess their faith in Jesus, these guides would be handed out to assist in building upon their faith, long after the tent had been torn down and the crusade moved on to Modesto for the next rally.

Seeing Billy up on the platform, Charles shouted, "What's buzzin', cousin? Have you given any more thought to what we talked about last night?" Charles asked Billy.

"I don't know Charles," Billy said indecisively. "I'm the president of Northwestern Bible College and going back to school to get an advance theological degree at Princeton? I just don't see that as a step forward right now," Billy replied.

"We'd be roommates. It would be killer-diller," Charles coaxed him. "You keep thinking about it, and after the meeting tonight we'll get a soda at the drug store and talk more about it. I'm not going to leave you alone until you say yes." Still looking around for the box of pamphlets, Charles added, "I guess I left the study guides at the church. I have to go there anyway and tell the choir director to have the choir sing 'Just as I am' as soon as we give the call to commit to Jesus. In fact, Billy, why don't you close out the rally tonight? You're better at getting a response than I," he turned to leave. "Remember now! I'm going to snap my cap if you say no about Princeton."

Peter continued to place chairs out but noticed a worried look on Billy's face. When Billy left the platform and came down to help Peter with the last row of chairs, Peter asked him, "What do you think of Robert Griffin?"

"Robert Griffin?" Billy questioned with a frown. "I don't believe I know him."

"He's quite famous," Peter said, while straightening the last chair. "He holds the record for having more degrees than anyone else in the world. But then again, maybe his professors know of him more than the average man does. The admissions office accounting department probably likes him a good bit too!" he said laughing before looking Billy straight in the eyes. "You have a gift, Billy Graham. If a gift stays wrapped in pretty paper for a year and then a bow is added to it another year later, who will ever know what's inside that beautiful, dusty package? How many souls will be denied God's gift of salvation while you sit in an auditorium with 50 other students listening to academics tell you what you could have been saying to thousands of people? Huh!" he chuckled. "Now *that* seems more like a math problem to me," he said turning back to survey the chairs one last time. "Maybe you should go to Princeton and study math?" he said with a twinkle of jest in his eye. "While there, you might run into Robert Griffin, the famous student that no one has ever heard of."

MEETING AT MATTHEW STREET

Later that day Billy Graham turned down Charles Templeton's offer to return to school and the end sum of that math equation meant that 3.2 million people responded to Billy and accepted Jesus Christ as their personal savior. And Charles? Nine years later in 1957, after struggling greatly with doubt, Charles announced to the world that he had become an agnostic, professing that he was incapable of providing sufficient rational grounds to justify either the belief that God exists or does not exist.

How sad, because Libby knew what Charles didn't. God does exist!

She picked up the next volume. It was marked, Andrew.

Andrew had been a tax collector. Due to the extravagances of the Roman rulers for construction, luxuries and perversions, taxes were forever increasing and the burden became much too great for the average citizen. Andrew knew this and had a heart for those who were struggling. Unlike other tax collectors, who took more than what was required and placed the extra money in their own greedy pockets, Andrew looked for ways to help the poor. As a result of this quest, he became friends with Amos before his death and resurrection.

Amos, had been a wealthy land owner who had groves of figs and olives, as well as fields of wheat and barley. Amos would not only allow the poor to glean, or pick late ripening crops from his land after it had undergone harvesting, but he worked with Andrew to help the poor pay their taxes that they couldn't afford so they would not get into trouble with the authorities.

Andrew was presently working for the IRS in a capacity allowing him to assist the members of the twelve blend in by obtaining identification and documents to support their current identities. Like James, he worked to promote good over evil by working from the inside of an organization where corruption was taking hold.

As a land owner in his first life, Amos not only took satisfaction in helping people with their taxes, but he enjoyed delighting in the culinary senses by creating delicious sauces, dips and baked goods out of the many foods that he harvested from his properties. With his wealth, he could import aromatic spices from far off lands and incorporate them into his many epicurean creations.

His unparalleled gift for combining flavors from multiple cultures placed him in high demand over the centuries amongst the rich and powerful. Currently, as head chef at the White House, he came into contact with heads of state from all over the world and spent many an hour in deep conversations with presidents who wandered into his kitchen on nights when they suffered from bouts of insomnia. He always offered wisdom that soothed the troubled mind.

Wives of leaders also come to Amos, marveling over his mastery of their own language to discuss recipes, cooking techniques, and on occasion issues that bore heavily upon their own hearts. He made everyone feel comfortable in communicating with him and any observations he shared were always well received.

It was Amos who retrieved their most prized possession, the podium upon which they kept their family Bible. He was the cook who made sure the French Revolutionary troops and their prisoners of war did not starve while they occupied the Cologne Cathedral in 1797. He was the one who saved the beautifully crafted podium from being used as firewood that night by replacing the warmth from the wood with a hot meal in the bellies of the prisoners.

Libby enjoyed trading recipes with Amos. But for Andrew, she always tried to let him know how important he was to the group. She understood that he felt the most unappreciated at times and always made sure he got unexpected gifts in the mail from her. His favorite were her lemon bars.

Moving onto the next two volumes she had to smile.

Of course, David, also known as Dr. D., and Jeremiah, better known as Jerry, basically did what they had always done together as a team. David was a doctor with a heart for helping children. In fact, he'd died from tuberculosis which he had contracted from one of his young patients. Jerry had originally been a builder in Sepphoris, a cosmopolitan city in the region of Galilee. He never cut corners on the quality of his work or the materials that he promised he would be using. He worked with integrity and demanded that everyone who worked with him observe the same moral standards over their work.

Throughout time David and Jerry became known as the original "Odd Couple" of the group. They spent more time together as a working team than any of the others. David normally worked in some rather remote areas and needed a facility from which he could provide his medical services. Jerry was always at the ready to renovate or construct whatever David and the community needed in the way of medical facilities, wells with better drinking water, or educational facilities where lives could be lifted and bad health habits corrected.

Libby loved the fact that they got along so well because they were so opposite from one another! David was organized. Everything had a place and once it was used, it was returned to its place. He was clean, as a matter of his profession, and he was gentle with children.

Jerry, on the other hand, was rough and gruff in looks and in speech. He was the only one in the group from whom foul language was tolerated. He tried to hold his tongue particularly when around Libby. But my heavens! The way he kept or *didn't* keep house could only be described as a disaster. Clothing everywhere. Tools everywhere. Empty wrappers left out. Shirts hung over the tops of open doors. He was a disaster in the home, but a genius on the job.

Libby resisted the temptation when visiting them to tidy up after Jerry. She accepted the fact that he was an adult and had his own unique idiosyncrasies. Regardless of his faults surrounding his untidy house, he did manage to maintain a clean and safe job site. Just as David could be attributed with saving tens of thousands of lives, Jerry deserved the same recognition. Whether it was a fight against smallpox and malaria, or erecting temporary clinics for treating Ebola, he and David were on a mission to save lives, no matter the cost while working in some of the worst places around the globe.

Now that they were working in New Orleans, they were feeling a tad guilty. It was a "pretty cushy gig" as Jerry called it in comparison to some of their previous missions. But they needed to have a break from the locations where they were becoming so well known for their life saving work in third world countries.

The fact that David and Jerry often rented an apartment together elevated David to the level of sainthood in Libby's eyes for being able to deal with Jerry's mess. But they really were a great team!

MEETING AT MATTHEW STREET

Libby got up to make sure she was not needed in the kitchen before returning to her last few volumes.

The next volume was quite large. Marcus had been a respected potter and businessman in Jerusalem. He had the most thankful heart that Libby had ever witnessed. Even when something went wrong in business, his response would always be a prayer to God thanking Him that it could have been much worse. Then he'd thank God for the lessons learned from the failure.

His outstanding business acumen meant he was the most diverse person in their group, having held the widest range of careers over time. He was instrumental in setting up all of the orphanages, halfway houses, hiring, training, and administering financial aid to each of their missions.

He had a forgiving spirit and never held a grudge. The people he loved most were the most unlovable, grumpy people. His acceptance of them caused them to turn introspectively and long to mirror him in their own lives, eventually becoming better people as a result.

Libby always passed ideas by Marcus to get his opinion before making decisions that affected the group. He was very wise.

Now Libby opened the volume for Phillip. He was her strong willed child. Because of his past, she knew she couldn't guide him. She opted only to support him as he dealt with a difficult job that she didn't want to know too much about. It was too horrifying for her to be made fully aware of the vile nature of the men Phillip worked at destroying.

Phillip had been a shepherd in his first life, but resented his job. He longed to be a soldier and travel the world, but as an only child he obeyed his parents and tended to the family's flock after his father died, leaving him to support his mother. He was a devoted son, nevertheless, and lived a life of service to his family.

In recent years, however, he worked in law enforcement and was deeply involved in staking out places where it was suspected that sex trafficking rings were operating. It disgusted him to the point of actually retching when he saw what was happening to innocent children and runaways. There were debase international businesses that sold underage minors to perverted politicians and wealthy businessmen from locations based all over the world. It was his mission to close down as many operations as possible and remove the offenders from society so they could no longer hurt anyone again.

Libby's heart broke for Phillip and what he had to endure. She often rubbed his temples or gave him back rubs. His shoulders were always as hard as a rock from the built up stress and tension that he was unable to release. It was obvious to her that he internalized his job and she wished she knew of a way to take his mind off the wickedness he was being exposed to incessantly. She often commandeered him to go to the movies with her to see a comedy. She felt like these were perhaps the only few hours this dedicated man might ever get when his mind was not tormented with the visions of horror that his job required him to witness. She drew his volume to her breast and said a prayer for peace for him.

And then there was precious Mara. Libby's heart broke as she examined Mara's tragic past.

MEETING AT MATTHEW STREET

CHAPTER FIFTEEN

Mara had been a weaver and sold handmade garments in the market place. She was outstandingly beautiful. She had an olive complexion, shiny thick black hair and large captivating eyes that were a remarkable amber color. As she walked through the market amongst her fellow vendors, people would do a double take as she passed by because of her rare beauty and graceful stride.

After one of her market days had come to a close, she was leaving town to head home. Her day had been particularly profitable. She only had a few pieces of her work that she had been unable to sell which she was bringing back home with her. One of the pieces was an exquisite sash which was dyed purple. Because the dye for this item was more difficult and costly to acquire, the long sash had not been affordable to most of the shoppers. There was one particularly wealthy woman, however, who showed a lingering interest in it and Mara felt certain she would return to her and purchase the sash the next time she returned and set up in the market place.

Mara lived a mile outside of town and she was almost home when she was passed by a Roman soldier on horseback named Lucius.

Lucius was quite disgruntled that day. His normal post was in Caesarea but he had been ordered to go to the market in Sepphoris and meet a vendor who dealt in Asian products from the trade guild. His superior had ordered him to go there and pick up a package that needed to be delivered to Emperor Tiberius.

Lucius felt he was above being used as a simple errand boy and this assignment hurt his ego greatly.

Over the years Lucius had moved up the ranks by first describing his superiors in such glowing terms that they'd be promoted. This in turn would leave an open position for him to be elevated. This method of advancement worked several times to his favor, but it seemed like his progression had come to a halt under his current commander. He believed that if he could just be relocated to Jerusalem, he could again get back on track climbing the ladder within the Roman military as he aspired to do.

His commander had been evasive regarding the parcel Lucius had been sent to pick up, so out of curiosity after acquiring the goods, he brought them into the inn where he would be spending the night. Carefully, he unwrapped the parcel so it wouldn't look tampered with. Once opened, he found within the wrappings several compounds; aphrodisiacs from the Orient meant for sexual virility. These sat atop a picture book, exquisitely painted, but filled only with sexually explicit scenes the nature of which Lucius had never seen nor could he have ever imagined.

With disgust he thought, "*This* is what my commander has sent me to pick up and deliver to Emperor Tiberius on the Island of Capri?" At first Lucius was even angrier about his assignment than before until he began to consider the potential of what he held in his hands. Blackmail, perhaps? A private meeting with a perverted emperor from whom he might request a reassignment? He would have to give this some further thought regarding ways to make this errand work more perfectly to his favor.

The following day when he found himself on the outskirts of Sepphoris he hadn't decided fully on a plan, until he passed Mara on the Roman road leaving town. He barely noticed the woman on foot walking ahead of him until he passed and looked back in her direction and noticed her beauty. Suddenly, Lucius was struck with an epiphany. He quickly pulled the reigns on his steed. When the horse circled back to face the oncoming Mara, he knew *exactly* what he would do.

"Carry my load," he demanded from Mara.

Mara looked bewildered, then looked behind her to see who else might be on the road with them. There was no one else in sight.

"You have a horse. You don't need me to carry anything," she observed.

"The law requires you to carry my load for one mile," he commanded as his spirited steed pranced in place.

The law did indeed required this of her. Even though Mara could see her home from where he had stopped her, his demand meant she would have to go with the soldier a mile beyond her house, and then walk a mile back to get home again. It was the law. She knew he was abusing it by making this outrageous request, but what else could she do? She stood before him and remained silent.

Lucius reached into his satchel and withdrew some dried fish wrapped in a pouch which he handed to Mara and told her to carry it. She was disgusted with this soldier. There was no need for her to have to comply with such a ridiculous request. He was only doing it because she thought he was trying to be funny at her expense.

Nevertheless, she had to obey the law.

Mara began to walk alongside Lucius and his horse as they got further and further from town. When they had reached the end of her mandatory mile, Lucius dismounted, took the pouch of fish from her and neatly replaced it back in his satchel. Then he commanded Mara, who had already turned to go home to, "Stop!"

Mara was not amused. What did he want now?

Lucius made sure no one was within sight and with a quick sweep of his foot, he hooked her legs out from under her. Mara fell hard to the stone paved road, and the breath got knocked out of her. He then made quick work of tying her wrists and feet together. When she wouldn't stop screaming he searched through her belongings and located her prized purple sash. He used this as a gag around her mouth and loaded her across the back of his horse.

If he wanted to request a favor from Emperor Tiberius, he thought of no better way to find favor with a sex crazed ruler than to bring him a gift of one of the most beautiful women he'd ever come across.

Suddenly, being an errand boy was turning into his best hope for promotion yet and he set off with Mara to catch a boat for the long journey to the Island of Capri.

MEETING AT MATTHEW STREET

CHAPTER SIXTEEN

Some might suggest that Emperor Tiberius was a victim of circumstances beyond his control or certainly outside of his preferences. But how could a person turn so vile if they were not deeply flawed to begin with?

No, he didn't want to become the Emperor. Yes, he was forced to divorce a wife whom he loved in order to marry a perverted, sexually immoral woman who was forced on him for political reasons. And yes, the wife that he had loved, was so disturbed by the process of divorce that she lost their second child before she could give birth.

Forcing leadership upon Tiberius destroyed his life. But why did that have to bring him to the point of destroying all the other lives he came into contact with?

For numerous reasons Tiberius decided to leave Rome. Rome was where he was sought after constantly by people wanting favors. Rome was where he had to account for his decisions that made some people want to shower him with accolades, while simultaneously causing others to plot his assassination. To escape it all, Tiberius decided that the only way to separate himself from the mayhem, surrounding him in Rome, was to relocate to an island in the Mediterranean called the Island of Capri.

One would think that the beauty and serenity of such a breathtaking setting would be enough to fill the soul with peace and fullness. But instead of drinking in the beauty of nature surrounding him, Tiberius drank in copious amounts of wine, leaving him in a constant state of intoxication.

Tiberius could have spent his days ruling from the splendor surrounding him in his finely crafted villa filled with works of art and luxury. Instead, he chose to entertain himself and his guests with orgies that took place throughout the Villa Jovis in specially designed nooks meant for promiscuity and nymphomania. Furthermore, Tiberius liked to watch boys dressed in costumes like that of the pagan god Pan copulating with one another in his gardens before he would invite them to swim with him naked in one of his pools while the young kidnapped boys pleased him sexually. Tiberius was so lewd in wanting his sex slaves to perform to his liking that he hired a trainer for them.

This trainer had the title of "Master of Imperial Pleasures." So, when Lucius landed on the shore of the Island of Capri with a woman bound and gagged, the dock workers didn't even ask the purpose of his visit before directing him to the Master's office.

Upon entering, the Master raised his eyes from the ledger over which he was working and took in the sight of Lucius and his female prisoner with mild interest regarding these unexpected guests.

"What is the nature of your visit?" the Master inquired.

"I was sent by my commander to deliver this parcel to the Emperor," Lucius said while handing over the package of aphrodisiacs and pornography.

The Master opened the parcel and brushed the bottled compounds aside in order to get a better look at the book that had just arrived from the orient. It had been long awaited and perhaps would rival even the explicit books he had already acquired from Egypt. Eagerly, he flipped through several pages and momentarily neglected the fact that Lucius and his hostage were still awaiting further recognition.

"I wasn't expecting anything more than these. What is this?" he asked nodding toward Mara as he got up from his desk. He walked over to Mara and while Lucius spoke, the Master encircled Mara twice, looking at her closely from head to toe. Ending his inspection, he stood facing her. Expressionless, he took his finger and casually flicked the end of the purple sash which bound her.

"The parcel is from my commander, but this rare woman of beauty is a gift to the Emperor from me, if he would consider hearing my request to have my post transferred from Caesarea to Jerusalem," Lucius explained.

Now the master encircled Lucius and inspected his physique. He considered asking Lucius to strip to the waist in order to see his muscles, but the breastplate he wore was sufficiently impressive and left something to the imagination regarding what might be beneath.

With a snap of his fingers, the Master called up his assistant and ordered him to take both Lucius and Mara away to be bathed.

"Your petition to take an audience with the Emperor is approved, but you will follow my precise instructions when doing so. I can't guarantee that your request will be granted," he said looking at Mara. "It depends on if he likes your offering or not."

The Master of Imperial Pleasures knew it was just as likely that the soldier would never make it off the island.

He had delivered the desired goods and Tiberius had an awful way of keeping knowledge of his hideous debauchery from making its way back to the mainland by simply eliminating his visitors. It was nothing for Tiberius to order sex slaves as well as his visitors thrown off the cliff on the east end of the island. He seemed to take just as much pleasure in his sexual perversions as he did in torturing people of all ages before watching them fall to an inevitable death below on the rocks.

An hour later when Lucius was brought back to the Master he was freshly bathed, hair combed, and his uniform was shining. The Master reached up and tousled Lucius's hair some to make him appear more rugged. Then the Master proccedeed to give him his instructions.

He was to lead Mara in to see the emperor using her purple sash like a leash around her neck. The sash had been tied in a slip knot that would tighten if she tried to get away from him.

He would only be allowed to speak when the emperor acknowledged him and he could only speak one sentence. After that, he would be expected to do anything and everything the emperor instructed him to do.

Lucius agreed and was led out of the staff quarters of the villa and into the more opulent areas where he passed erotic statues and massive columns. His footsteps echoed as they made their way to the place where Tiberius would be found.

The guards stopped outside two massive doors with elaborate wood carvings and inlay on them as an entourage came toward them from the other end of the great hallway. Being led by this group was Mara. Her amber eyes were framed in red from crying, and she smelled of the wine which had been administered to her as a means to subdue her. She had been stripped naked and dressed in a flowing, transparent gown. Under the gown she was wearing colorful jewelry that crisscrossed her breasts and clasped in the back. One of her handmaidens placed the free end of the purple sash tied to Mara's neck into Lucius's hand and the immense doors were then opened.

Lucius entered with Mara as two guards and Mara's handmaidens entered behind them.

Seated in front of them was Tiberius. To his left was a side table with a chalice of wine and a plate piled high with fruit and various cheeses. Squatting to his right like a faithful dog was a boy of approximately 8 years of age who wore the tanned skin of a leopard strapped to his body like a costume. The boy was fully naked beneath the skin that was draped over his back. The sight of the child's exposed genitalia as he squatted there made Lucius uncomfortable and he began to think that his offering of a beautiful woman would not win him the favors he sought. Occasionally, Tiberius would reach over and stroke the top of the boy's head who would then nuzzle him back. Occasionally, the boy would lift his hand and lick at it like a cat would lick his paw.

They remained awkwardly standing before Tiberius for several minutes before the silence was finally broken.

"Speak," Tiberius barked.

"Your Imperial Majesty, I hail from a post in Caesarea and offer you this gift in the hope you would grant my petition for reassignment to Jerusalem." That was all Lucius was allowed to speak based upon his instructions.

Tiberius barely looked at Mara. He was more interested in Lucius's biceps that barely peeked out from below the sleeve of his tunic. Then his eyes lingered on the large calf muscles that appeared above his laced sandals.

"Caesarea. They worship Pan there," Tiberius stated, directing his comment toward Lucius who didn't dare reply to this accurate statement.

Tiberius then motioned for one of the guards and directed him to send in the Master of Imperial Pleasures to come speak with him.

"Take them to holding," he directed his staff. Mara was led away by the handmaidens and Lucius went with the guards.

A half hour passed before Lucius was taken to a balcony overlooking the most exquisite garden he'd ever seen. The balcony was in a "U" shape and was filled with Tiberius's guests. They were all quite drunk and talking loudly amongst themselves. When Tiberius entered and took his place at the centermost place of the balcony, his guests cheered for him and offered toasts to his good fortune.

In the garden below stood his Master of Imperial Pleasures and with a nod of Tiberius' head, the Master exited the garden while dozens of young boys dressed in costumes to look like Pan came running in and took up places hiding in various parts of the garden below.

Next, dozens of young girls ran in and danced hither and thither dressed as nymphs while one child guided Mara to the center of the garden where she stood, blindfolded by her purple sash.

The spectators fell silent, breathlessly awaiting the next moment when Mara's eyes would be uncovered and the spectacle would begin.

MEETING AT MATTHEW STREET

As the blindfold was removed, great shouts erupted from the observation decks in the balcony while Mara allowed her eyes to adjust to her new surroundings. With that, the girls began to taunt her, pulling at her hair and tugging at her arms while some bit her causing her to scream out and try to run away. Apparently, the game was to make her run past the hiding places of the young boys at their stations. As soon as she got close to where one was, the boy would become "free" to join in the pursuit of Mara. So, the more she ran, the more she unleashed those who would join in tracking her and hunting her down.

Children are easy for an adult to shake off. Dozens of children, however, can subdue an adult and that is what was expected in the game that was unfolding below.

Once Mara was unable to get away from the throngs of children, a frenzy broke out. The boys began to have their way with her and each other as the nymph dressed girls held her at bay. Mara struggled unsuccessfully with her molesters. Meanwhile, the crowd watching from above went berserk. Couples began to copulate with one another as the balcony erupted into a freakishly crazed orgy.

Lucius became so repulsed by all that he was seeing that he turned away from the madness and saw the face of his emperor, aglow with satisfaction over the turmoil he had orchestrated.

Standing by Tiberius' side, Lucius could contain his repulsion no longer and retched. When Tiberius saw Lucius's reaction and smelled the sour reek of vomitus, he became disgusted with what would have been his next toy of the evening. This man was weak. How dare he offer a gift and then decide how that gift might be enjoyed by the recipient.

Tiberius motioned for the Master, now standing beside him waiting for instructions. "Prepare the leap," he instructed with a flick of his hand.

The Master exited to gather the guards for what would happen next.

Many of the guests retreated to other areas to indulge in the pleasures of the young actors who had performed in the garden below while Tiberius took Lucius out to the east cliff of the island. A breeze was coming up the side of the bluff while a sunset silhouetted them from behind.

Standing in a line were five children who had just been brought there from the garden molestation. Standing next to them was Mara, covered in scratches, bite marks and bleeding. Her handmade purple sash was once again tied around her long neck. Lucius recognized one of the children who had not participated in the horrid sex game, but had only stood in a corner of the garden crying. She was a beautiful little girl with hair of golden ringlets.

One by one Tiberius reveled in watching the children as they were thrown over the edge of the bluff, listening to their fading screams until they abruptly ended below. Evidently these captives had not performed with the type of gusto that Tiberius found to be acceptable. Now they would never be able to recount their time spent on his island and reveal the atrocities taking place there.

After the fifth child had been eliminated by the long, 1000 foot fall from the cliff face, all eyes turned to Mara who would soon be lifted, kicking and screaming as all of his previous victims had. She would surely meet her fate the same way as each of the previous children had.

MEETING AT MATTHEW STREET

"My lovely," Tiberius said looking upon Mara for the last time, "it's time to call upon your precious god Pan to catch you at the bottom of the rocks below." Then Tiberius changed the pitch of his voice to that of a woman and mockingly he cried out, "Save me! Save me Pan!" and he laughed at his own taunting.

With that, Mara professed proudly, "My God is *not* Pan! My God is the one true God. The almighty Jehovah!" With that she broke free from the guards and instead of running from the edge of the cliff, she willfully ejected herself over the edge without a sound, leaving the astounded Tiberius in her wake.

In a red faced rage Tiberius lunged at Lucius grabbing him by the neck. "She was a Jew!? You said you were from Caesarea!"

"I am!" cried Lucius in a choked voice. "I came across her while leaving Sepphoris where I picked up your parcel," he explained with bewilderment. What was this perverse man's issue? He had absolutely no morals whatsoever, and now he's asking about and concerned over this woman's religious beliefs? He's an absolute madman, Lucius thought!

Tiberius backhanded Lucius across the face and before Lucius could react, guards were holding him back by his arms. "I have to think. I have to think," Tiberius said, pacing back and forth while holding his head in his hands.

Turning to the Master he demanded, "Get me the astrologer!"

Looking again at Lucius he shouted while wagging his finger squarely in his face, "You! You! ... You have brought her God's wrath upon me!"

Lisa Kirkman

Tiberius had always protected the Jews and their religious beliefs. He demanded that people like Pontius Pilate allow them to follow their customs and not get cross ways with them. For a man who was concerned more about keeping wine in his cup and lust in his heart, it was surprising that he admired the Jew's religious customs to the extent that he did and that he maintained a healthy dose of fear of their God.

Tiberius retained an astrologer who lived on the island with him and even had an observatory built there to suit his soothsaying needs. He explained to the astrologer what had just happened and demanded that he read the stars that night to see how the death of such a devout Jew at his hands might potentially affect him.

Before sending Lucius to his death over the cliff, he decided to keep him alive, at least until morning so his next move could be based upon whatever the astrologer might reveal to him.

That night, Tiberius could not sleep. He drank heavily, trying to ease his mind, but the more he drank, the more he thought he saw dark figures coming toward him while the room spun in his head. These dark figures wished to attack him in ways far worse than those who plotted his assassination on the mainland. He was crazed with worry.

When morning finally arrived, the astrologer was ready to report his findings. Tiberius braced himself for the news.

"The Jewish woman who jumped was an exceptionally righteous believer in her God," he reported. "The stars say that she will live a long life, which confuses me. The stars, however, were quite clear that she should be given a proper Jewish burial. I am confused by the contradictory messages I'm getting. Therefore, I think you should dispatch a team immediately to see if she survived the fall. If she didn't, then she needs to be buried in Jerusalem with full honors performed by their high priest Caiaphas."

"What about the soldier who brought her here? Should I have him killed?" Tiberius inquired.

"No. Use him to retrieve the woman and see to her proper burial. Then grant him whatever it was he was requesting so he will remain quiet about what he has seen here," the astrologer instructed.

Based on the advice of his astrologer, Tiberius gave the order to his fleet commander to ready the boats and escort Lucius to the foot of the cliff. He was not to be allowed to leave the island unless he recovered Mara's body.

Tiberius's heart pounded inside of his chest. What if she was alive? What then? He anxiously awaited word to be relayed back to him as he watched the boats launching from the northern shore with Lucius who was desperate to leave this island of Hades. He had planned to jump overboard if he was unable to find Mara's body. Better to drown in the Gulf of Naples than to suffer at the hands of the tyrannical emperor.

Because of rough seas and a rocky shoreline, upon reaching the bottom of the cliff, a smaller boat had to be dispatched with several oarsmen and Lucius. When the boat could get no closer, Lucius stripped off his clothes and was lowered overboard with a rope tied around his waist. Waves lifted his body up high before crashing it down again upon the outcropping of rocks. Over and over again he struggled to find footing on the rough shore. When he was finally able to stand, he fell repeatedly on the slippery rocks before making it to dryer land.

The stench of rotting flesh was overpowering. A throng of sea birds pecking at the flesh of the children from the night before made it difficult to see the shore underneath their outstretched, angrily flapping wings as they postured toward one another demanding their space amongst the fresh batch of meat.

Lucius scoured the rocky base, kicking at the birds who refused to move out of his way between spasms of painful dry heaves from the overwhelming stench. While kicking aside one of the clusters, he slipped on the slime from one of the decomposing bodies, fell and hit his head on a rock. For a few moments he felt dizzy and disoriented. The images before him were blurred while his brain worked to process through the massive jolt he'd just received. As his sight came back into focus he discovered that he had landed face to face with the macabre figure of a child whose hollow eye sockets had been pecked and eaten out. He jerked with a start! Horror stricken, he realized that plastered across one cheek were the blood caked ringlets that had appeared golden only the day before. The precious, crying child would cry no more. Lucius lay motionless for a moment, mortified. It was a sight that would bring humans to their knees and angels to tears. However, it was from this new perspective that he was able to catch the slightest glimpse of a purple color being trampled beneath webbed feet. It was Mara's purple sash.

Shooing more birds away he uncovered her lifeless body. Full rigor mortis had set in and he dragged her like a dried piece of rawhide across shards of rock to the water's edge. Had she not been in full rigor, her body would have draped over his arm like a blanket. All of her bones had shattered on impact.

Upon getting her onto the larger boat that would take them to the mainland, Lucius took out the bedroll from his gear and gently covered her rigid body with it. As he looked down upon the sight, he fell to his knees beside her, weeping uncontrollably, screaming out from deep within his soul with guilty wailing over the atrocities that he had just witnessed and the fact that he had made them all possible.

Lisa Kirkman

CHAPTER SEVENTEEN

Libby closed the volume marked for Mara. Was there any wonder why she held her close to her heart?

Mara worked closely with Phillip and his mission to shut down human trafficking rings. She, like Libby, shielded herself from the horrific stories, but she dedicated all of her art proceeds to aiding Phillip's work.

Until Christianity was legalized in 313 AD, her art was limited to the walls of house churches, private residences where members of the risen twelve worked with small groups of people to spread their Christian message. Most of these works didn't stand the test of time and were forever lost.

Three hundred years later her work appeared in illuminated manuscripts, highly detailed borders or marginalia surrounding text. Since some of these works were done on papyrus, they disintegrated over time while her body did not. For this reason, her current work was always done with longevity in mind, using the finest paints and the most impervious substrates.

She never took part in writing the actual text of the manuscripts within her detailed marginalia, however, for three reasons. One, she had horrible penmanship for an artist. Two, the writing of text was often only allowed by monastic scribes who underwent detailed rituals when writing the text. The rituals, however, were not nearly as strict as had been required of Jewish scribes when writing the Old Testament. Those scribes were required to wipe the pen and wash their bodies each time before writing the word God.

The third reason she didn't write the text was because she was a woman. That's not to say, however, that many of her commissioned works were not done under male pseudonyms throughout the centuries in order to circumvent any gender discrimination.

Women in her first life were not as subjugated or subservient to men as they were to become in later years. She had owned her own business in her first life and was a powerful, respected woman in her community. Proverbs 31 described a woman of noble character in her first life as strong, working with her hands, acquiring food from far off, managing the hired hands, able to enter into contracts to buy land and then cultivate the property, turning it into a profit making endeavor. The woman described in the Old Testament was not a woman who was being oppressed by the men in her life. She was a formidable, equal, and capable person. Mara sometimes struggled with being "put in her place" in her resurrected life when various cultures took a turn toward a more misogynistic viewpoint.

As Libby lovingly replaced all the diaries in their place next to her chair in the meeting room, she could smell Amos's cooking wafting in. She was very grateful to be treated to a meal that she did not have to prepare for everyone else.

Upon entering the kitchen, Libby noticed a large bowl on the counter which was now almost overflowing with outgoing mail. Now that everyone had returned, they had evidently brought essential paperwork home with them.

She saw several payments of bills, including one for Jefferson Parish Water Department for Jerry and David's water bill. There were letters to missionaries who they were supporting, and she knew one large envelope contained portions of a manuscript rewrite and signed contract that Simon was working on with his publisher. That one would need to be sent by registered return receipt. She made a mental note to go to the post office tomorrow.

CHAPTER EIGHTEEN

Robert Stellman sat in his car with a newspaper opened before him. Even with the seat run all the way back, he was still cramped. On the seat next to him lay a stack of magazines. North American Whitetail, American Rifleman and American Hunter. In his cup holder were the remainders of an icy drink he'd been nursing since lunch. He loved the sweetness of the slushy drinks, but he hated the brain freeze they gave him. The portion that was now left in the bottom of the cup was a hard, colorless and tasteless slush. He was drinking the Piña Colada flavor today and considered buying two more at quitting time. He wanted to share one with Angela, his girlfriend, to see if it would mix well with some dark rum to make a frozen cocktail. It was Friday and he was ready to see the Post Office stakeout come to an end for the week, but they unfortunately would be open for a half day again on Saturday. At least he'd get *somewhat* of a break over the weekend, but not much.

As he turned to the sports section, he saw a car pull up to the small Post Office. He casually took notice of it. He had witnessed hundreds of visitors already, with none of them matching the description he was after. But when he glanced up a few more times his interest began to pique when he noticed that no one was getting out at first. They appeared to be making movements inside the car, maybe reaching for mail, maybe a purse, or a parcel…or… with that he saw movements that would indicate the person inside was wrapping their head in a scarf.

Lisa Kirkman

Stellman threw the paper down on the seat and grabbed a pair of binoculars next to him. He could clearly see that it was someone tying a scarf around their head and checking their image in the rear view mirror before getting out with a plastic bag filled with letters.

He quickly started his car and pulled in next to Libby's car outside of the small Post Office.

Libby went inside with her bag of mail and placed the smaller loose pieces through a slot marked "OUT OF TOWN." Then she stood at the main counter and waited for the young man who worked there to realize she was there.

As she waited, Stellman walked in and began filling out a green USPS Tracking form on the counter behind her. Libby briefly looked over her shoulder at him before turning back toward the service counter.

When the postal worker came out of his side room and saw her, he took in a quick breath of surprise, and immediately looked to the other end of the front office where he saw Stellman working with his fake forms. The worker cleared his throat loudly and Stellman shook his head in disbelief. Of course, he knew this was the woman. Why would he be in there otherwise? Stellman kept his head down and continued to write, ignoring the postal worker.

"I'd like you to stamp the date on this return receipt letter for me please," Libby requested. She liked to see the postal mark being made in person. Trust but verify. She never took chances with important matters.

She noticed the young man behind the counter seemed peculiarly different today. He was normally so laid back that he almost appeared to be struggling to keep his eyes open. But today, however, they appeared alert and they were darting this way and that. Just looking at him made her nervous. She again looked over her shoulder at the man behind her and began to get an uneasy feeling. Phillip called it spider senses.

After the postal worker tore off her green and white return receipt and handed it back to her for tracking, Libby went to their oversized mail drawer and used her key to open it. It was so full that she had to press down on the contents to allow the drawer to open more freely. Squatting next to the box, she emptied the contents into the plastic bag she had come in with. When she was finished, she looked back to see where Stellman was and realized he was no longer in the Post Office.

She left with her load of incoming mail and returned to her car where she removed her scarf and pulled away from the parking lot. Hers was the only car parked there.

A short distance up the street, Stellman had his car pulled to the side of the road and waited for Libby to start moving in whatever direction she would leave before giving her some space and falling in behind her.

Libby left the Post Office and began to return to the safe house using the route she always took making multiple turns and odd cut backs. But when she noticed a car in the distance that seemed to make a few of her unusual turns, she began to get suspicious and she sped up. Now she was making even more unusual turns and when Stellman saw that she was driving erratically, he called off the pursuit.

Libby felt flush. She began to sweat as her heart raced with fear. She was sure she was being followed. Something just didn't seem right to her. The postal worker, the mysterious man who didn't mail a letter, a car following her elusive path. She began to feel in her purse for her phone to call James and ask him what she should do when she realized she no longer saw the car following her. It appeared to have pulled into a driveway somewhere in the previous block. Still, Libby gripped the steering wheel firmly with both hands and added five more minutes to her route before returning home.

Stellman returned to the convenience store and filled two giant cups with Piña Colada slushies. When he got back in his car he phoned his girlfriend Angela and told her his stakeout was a success and he was headed her way.

Stellman pulled away from the convenience store and started toward Angela's apartment. Picking up his drink, he took a sip from the Piña Colada slushy, a sweet drink to celebrate his sweet success. Before replacing the drink back in the cup holder next to the one he'd also purchased for Angela, he raised his oversized Styrofoam cup and said out loud, "Cheers to a happy weekend!" he smiled, congratulating himself, as he made a toast toward his car's windshield and the weekend ahead of him.

He'd get with Ron on Monday to pull up the coordinates for where Libby ended up because he had attached a magnetic tracking device under her rear bumper before she left the Post Office. "Gotcha!"

MEETING AT MATTHEW STREET

CHAPTER NINETEEN

The next morning around 6:30 A.M. Aaron came down the stairs to find Libby, as he expected, enjoying a fresh cup of black coffee in the kitchen. She already had his favorite cup sitting out, waiting for him. It read, "Only LEFT-HANDED people are in their RIGHT minds."

They were always the ones to rise first. This was their special time for enjoying one another's company before the house came alive with the hustle and bustle that so many people in one space naturally created. Normally, full gatherings like this one only materialized on major holidays or just before planning a big move complete with new identities for everyone.

Aaron pulled out a backless bar stool from under the ledge of the kitchen's island and straddled the seat while Libby fixed his coffee with just the right amount of cream and sugar. While she prepared it, Aaron tapped a thick envelope he had brought down with him on the countertop in front of him.

Libby listened as she heard the sound of the sharp crack of the paper against the surface of the table before Aaron flipped it to its narrow edge. Tap-tap. Turn. Tap-tap. Turn.

Libby handed him his coffee and presumed that his nervous fidgeting was a sign that he was still upset from the conversation from the day before.

"You know, Aaron, your past life is not who you are now. It's what makes you a better person today, but you aren't that person any longer." Libby reassured him.

"Oh no. I know that. I just hope *other* people know that. But that's kinda why I wanted to give you this," he said sliding the envelope across the surface toward her.

The envelope was addressed to Aaron's Apple Foundation and their post office box address. That foundation was what they used for supporting educational causes. As Libby looked at the address, Aaron explained.

"That letter found me a few years back and I'd like it added to my diary if you wouldn't mind. It sort of goes along with what you just said and I'd like it kept as part of my permanent record," he requested of her as their official historian.

Libby smiled and said, "Consider it done!" and she gave the envelope her own, tap-tap against the island.

With that, Phillip and Jerry entered the kitchen and Libby looked surprised.

"You two are up early!" she exclaimed.

"Yep!" Jerry said clapping his hands and rubbing them together. Early rising was common for him on the construction site, but he normally allowed himself some extra sleep when they were all together. He continued, "Aaron and Phillip are gonna help me with the plumbing issues you were tellin' me about," he said, while grabbing a Coke out of the refrigerator. "We wanna knock it out early," he said opening the bottle. He then turned to Phillip and commanded like a job foreman, "Grab yourself some coffee so we can go out back and make a list of the supplies we'll need to buy."

After the men had filed out the back door, Libby opened Aaron's letter, removed the pages and began to flatten them as best as she could so the letter might fit more smoothly within the pages of Aaron's volume.

MEETING AT MATTHEW STREET

Libby topped off her coffee with enough coffee to heat what was left in the cup before going into the meeting room where she extracted Aaron's volume from her stack. She began to read the letter in order to decide where amongst the pages it might fit best. It read as follows in cursive handwriting:

To My Former Teacher or His Heirs,

I hope this letter finds you well. You won't remember me, but I felt compelled to send this letter, and this is why.

I'm 55 years old now. I was a student of yours 37 years ago when I was a senior at Seminole High School in 1979. I recently underwent surgery for uterine cancer and I'm taking a few days off while recovering. I feel sure it was caught in the early stages, but the word "cancer" always sounds so scary. Nevertheless, it makes you evaluate your life, where you've been and what you still have ahead of you.

So I decided to take this time while off from work to write thank you notes to the people in my life who changed it for the better. And guess what? You came to mind!

As a child I had always been considered a poor reader. I really wasn't, but my dad was dyslexic and my mom was so certain she would give birth to someone who would follow in my dad's shortcomings, that she projected her fears onto me. My best friend from High School still laughs at how I sighed deeply when I was asked to read the Bible out loud in Sunday school. It was only because I was so intimidated by Valerie Morgan, who could read like the guy at the end of a car commercial. I was embarrassed to be found out for my apparent reading disability.

Lisa Kirkman

So, as a senior I signed up for your speed reading class. I figured that there was a "trick" to reading fast and by golly, I was going to learn what that was. I remembered you had these microfiche films that scrolled on a screen, but imagine my horror when you handed out a list of books and informed us that we would be required to select and read five of these books by the end of the term! Read!? Five books!?

Luckily, I had read Animal Farm in a summer class for Comparative Political Systems, so I aced that book report right off the bat. But that still meant I had to read four more books.

I remember running to the school library in order to beat all the other students in your class, and with your list in hand I began measuring spines. If I was going to be forced to read four of those suckers, they were going to be as small as possible. As a result, I picked up a copy of Ayn Rand's book, Anthem. 42 pages? Awesome! But I have to tell you, they turned out to be 42 pages that changed my life! Those few pages launched me into a love of reading that allowed me to read her book, Fountainhead (720 pages), a plethora of the classics and later as a mom, all the Harry Potter books which I read out loud (without heavy sighing) to my daughter before she was old enough to read them herself.

Who would have ever guessed that a teacher's assignment and a 42 page book on that list would shape me into the person I am today? Again, I hope this letter finds you well. Please know that you are on my heart... Pardon me...I'm choked up just writing this. You are appreciated, you are remembered and I pray that this message gets to you. I can't thank you enough.

MEETING AT MATTHEW STREET

With sincere gratitude,
Laura Olsen, class of '79

Libby turned the pages of Aaron's volume and decided to slip it into the section just before the 1980's. She knew that Aaron must have read and reread that letter many times over the past four years since receiving it. She found it an honor to be able to include it in his history because where there was one person who came forward to say thank you, there were hundreds more who felt the same way, but just hadn't voiced it.

CHAPTER TWENTY

Aaron pushed a large H Cart filled with PVC and two-by-fours up aisle ten to where Jerry stood in front of a display of pull out trays. Jerry was studying each part intently while Phillip stood by Aaron's side waiting for Jerry's next command.

Further up the aisle were several rows that ran perpendicular to the aisle they were on and Phillip, who was always aware of his surroundings, noticed some unusual movement at the corner of aisle nineteen, a few rows up from where they stood.

At about waist height, he saw a head bob out from the corner before bobbing back out of sight. He observed it two more times before nudging Aaron with his elbow. With a silent cock of his head and movement of his eyes, he directed Aaron's attention to what he was seeing.

With that, a four year old Hispanic boy eased further around the corner while stealthily holding a caulking gun within his accurate grip, clearly aimed in their direction.

In Spanish, Aaron quickly shouted an old militia military command that meant to drop and roll from danger. Before they knew it, Jerry ducked and maneuvered skillfully and swiftly across the floor to the other side of the aisle, only to be met with hysterical laughter from Aaron and Phillip.

"You still got the moves old man!" Phillip taunted.

Jerry grasped at his heart and asked, "What the *hell*?"

MEETING AT MATTHEW STREET

Phillip turned to Aaron and said, "Good thing you have that cart between you and him. He'd probably pop you one if he could reach you!"

With that, Jerry, red faced and full of anger looked in the opposite direction to where the silicone wielding sniper still stood, slightly hunched, caulk gun at the ready until he saw the inflamed look on Jerry's face. Panic stricken, the child straightened as if he had taken the shock of an electrical jolt. Jerry's expression was so frightening to him that the boy promptly dropped the product to his feet, and walked his stiffened little body backwards around the corner until he was out of sight. Not for long, however, because a Hispanic male soon emerged and grabbed up the caulk gun from the floor with one hand while half dragging the boy up the aisle behind him, away from Jerry's direction. The young boy stumbled repeatedly trying to keep up with his father while straining not to take his eyes off of Jerry in case he might need to break free and run for it.

"Adios Gran Capitán!" Jerry yelled after the boy.

"Aw man! You saw it too?" Phillip marveled, slapping Jerry on the shoulder. "He was Gonzalo reincarnated. I swear. Don't you think, Aaron?"

"Why do you think I yelled the Spanish command like I did?" Aaron replied. "That kid looked exactly the way Gonzalo did at that age. *Exactly*!"

"Man! I thought there was an active shooter or something in the store the way you shouted that command. Shooo!" Jerry said rubbing his forehead. "And you're right, Phillip. Good thing I am praus and can keep my strength under control or I *would* pop Aaron for making me look like a darned fool!" Jerry said shifting his weight into a mock squaring off at Aaron.

Lisa Kirkman

"Clean up on aisle 10!" Phillip joked, pointing at Aaron.

"Wow! Yah know, it's amazing how it took me immediately back to our training routines!" Jerry laughed, shaking his head in disbelief. "I can't believe I did that. Talk about ingrained training!"

Smiling at his reaction, their minds drifted back to the year 1457. Phillip had been involved in the local militia training near Cordoba, Spain. It involved the training of young boys in the use of weapons of war. It was then that Phillip first came into contact with two brothers from a prominent family.

The eldest, Alonso, was in training with Phillip, but his younger brother was too young at the time to participate. Young Gonzalo attended, nevertheless, religiously standing on the sidelines using small limbs or branches to imitate his older brother's every move. As Alonso practiced lunges with a pike, little Gonzalo awkwardly did the same.

Phillip especially liked the boys and had empathy for them, because their father had died only two years earlier. Phillip knew very well the difficulties of growing up without a father, having been an only child and the sole supporter of his widowed mother in his first life.

Phillip reminisced about one particular, hot summer's day when the boys in training decided they would end the session with a swim in a nearby stream. Before leaving, however, many of the boys taunted four year old Gonzalo, poking him in his belly with their pikes.

"Go home to your mama little baby," Miquel goaded. "You can't swim, so go home!"

Gonzalo pouted and looked at the boys with contempt. Another boy, Ramon, took his pike and while

MEETING AT MATTHEW STREET

Gonzalo leaned against his makeshift weapon, he knocked Gonzalo's stick away at the base, causing Gonzalo to fall. Laughter erupted from all the boys as they pointed fingers at Gonzalo who sat on the ground crying until his brother Alonso reached down, helped him to his feet and brushed the dirt from his legs.

"You're ok. Don't pay attention to Ramon. He has to pick on children half his age," Alonso reassured Gonzalo. With that, the other boys pointed their fingers at Ramon and the laughter turned on him, instead.

Phillip thought it was wonderful how the older brother stood up for his younger sibling, refusing to bow to the peer pressure. So, after praising Alonso for being kind to his brother, and giving Ramon a stern look of admonition, Phillip offered to accompany them to the stream to keep an eye on the four year old so they could all have a good time without worrying about Gonzalo's safety.

As the older boys ran ahead, little Gonzalo reached up and took Phillip's hand as they walked. Immediately, Phillip's heart melted over this small act of trust in him as a protector. He knew he'd never be able to have a son of his own and the feeling of that tiny hand within his own was the beginning of what fueled his passion to help and protect all the children he himself would never be able to father or protect as his own.

As they approached the stream, they could hear a barrage of laughter coming from the boys who were already splashing wildly in the cool water. Phillip sat down on a rock and patted it. Gonzalo obediently perched next to him.

A minute later, Phillip wiped his brow and noticed that Gonzalo wiped his brow, too. Phillip scratched his right ankle. Gonzalo scratched his right ankle. Phillip swatted at a fly. Gonzalo swatted at an imaginary fly. Now Phillip was the one being imitated instead of the brother.

While watching the boys roughhouse, Phillip began to think out loud making note of what he was seeing. "Huh. Francisco has good upper body strength. Look how he flipped Pedro over his back. He'll make a good warrior."

"Aw, if only Rafael could fight as well as he swims! Of course, in battle I'd use him to swim a river with a line for the other men to hold onto. He might not be a warrior, but he has his own set of skills."

A few minutes later he pointed to another, "That one. He's a warrior too. He's just quiet and stealthy. He chooses when to attack without exhausting himself first."

"I want to be a warrior," Gonzalo said.

Phillip looked down at Gonzalo and saw there was clear potential in the young boy. He never missed a training session and Phillip often used him as an example to the older boys who wished to take a break when they were tired. Phillip gave it some thought and then slapped both hands on the top of his thighs before asking, "How would it be if I told you a story about a man who *didn't* want to be a warrior but God chose him to be one anyway? It's about a man named Gideon."

Gonzalo slapped both his hands on the top of his thighs and said, "Tell me."

"Well, Gideon had a problem with bullies."

"Like Ramon?" Gonzalo asked.

"Worse. Much worse. These bullies were called Midianites. They were so mean that Gideon and his people, called Israelites, had to hide from them. The Midianites ruined the crops, stole food, donkeys and sheep. They were very bad. But Gideon's people prayed to God to help them."

"So an angel appeared to Gideon." Upon hearing this, Gonzalo took his attention off of the boys at play and looked at Phillip in surprise. "Yes, an angel. And the angel told Gideon that he was a strong warrior. But Gideon said, no I'm not. Everyone in my family is more important than me!" Gonzalo shook his head in sympathetic agreement with Gideon's plight. "But then God got involved and told Gideon that He would make winning the battle against the bullies easy!"

"Gideon gathered men from all over to help him fight the Midianites, but God told him, you have too many men! Tell them that if anyone is scared, they should go home."

"Twenty-two thousand cowardly men ran home and left 10,000 soldiers behind. But God said that was *still* too many. You see, God wanted everyone to know that the Israelites were not powerful because of how many there were, but how strong their God was." Phillip stopped and tried to think of a way to describe the numbers to a four year old, so he drew squares in the fine gravel at their feet and called the tiny pebbles people.

"Then God told Gideon to take the remaining men to the spring," and he pointed to the boys playing in the water, "and test them." Gonzalo turned to Phillip and focused his fullest attention upon him to find out what the test might be. His interest was piqued.

"God told Gideon to observe how each man drank from the spring. Three hundred of them scooped the water into their cupped hands and then drank it, while all the rest got on their knees to drink. That's when God told Gideon to only keep the three hundred men for his army who drank from their cupped hands without getting onto their knees," and Phillip circled a tiny patch of pebbles. "This is 300. That's all he had in his army!" Phillip said while comparing the original number of pebbles to what was remaining.

Phillip was struck for a moment and reflected on his own thoughts. Three hundred people. Yet God felt that He could work through just the twelve elect of his group? It worried him. Was he doing God's will? Was he making the difference that he was supposed to be making?

Phillip shook the worry from his mind and continued, "So Gideon went from THIS, to this," he said pointing at the piles. Gonzalo's eyes widened. "Now, for me, I would say that the men who squatted and scooped the water, remained in a position that would allow them to move quickly if they had to. If a wild animal came at them or an enemy emerged from the tree line, the squatting men could spring away quickly," he said while shooting his arms up into the air. "They were always prepared. But the men who drank while on their knees? Well, they would not be able to react as quickly as the men who squatted to scoop the water up."

Phillip looked out at the boys playing. "Some people, very few, are always at the ready for whatever dangers might come their way."

"What happened next?" Gonzalo asked.

"Well, the number of the Midianites was like this entire shore of pebbles," Phillip said with a dramatic sweep of his arm across the shoreline. "That's how big their army was, but look," he pointed again to Gideon's tiny circle of pebbles, "this was all Gideon had on his side. So he separated the men into 3 groups and they surrounded the Midianites. Then they made lots of noise that made them sound like there were more of them than there really were and it upset the enemy so badly that they began to fight one another before they all ran off!" Phillip said, accentuating the end of the story with a grand clap of his hands.

Gonzalo laughed, jumped up and ran straight for the stream. Phillip assumed the young boy was simply pretending to be a fleeing Midianite, but when he got to the edge of the stream, he jumped into the deepest part and promptly flailed his arms and kicked with his little legs until he reached the other shore and climbed up the bank. Turning to the dumbfounded boys in the water he clinched his fists and screamed at them, "I'm a warrior too!"

Phillip was now standing at the edge of the stream, heart pounding wildly within his chest as he turned to Alonso. "I thought he couldn't swim?"

Alonso shrugged his shoulders.

Gonzalo said gleefully and out of breath as if there was nothing to what he had just done, "I watched Rafael and learned how to swim!" He then jumped back into the water with the other boys and played until Phillip had to carry him home, sleeping in his arms from exhaustion.

Forty six years later in 1503 Gonzalo, known as Gonzalo Fernandez de Cordoba, engaged the French army numbering 10,000 troops while leading his own 6,000 Spanish troops at the Battle of Cerignola. He arranged his men with the pikemen tightly packed in the center under Ramon's command (no longer a bully, but one of his most loyal soldiers). On one flank he positioned long guns called arquebusiers and on the other, his swordsmen. This was the first time in history that a battle was won primarily due to the use of firearms.

Gonzalo became known as El Gran Capitán having captured over 700 war trophy banners during his career. He was fearless, recklessly daring, but shrewd. His men would often find him before a battle, squatting and drawing squares and circles in the dirt while in deep contemplation…but he was never seen kneeling.

♦♦♦

Aaron loaded the last piece of PVC pipe into the back of Jerry's pickup truck on top of the lumber they had purchased while Jerry opened up the aluminum tool box that spanned the width of the truck bed. Time after time Jerry would withdraw a strap from the box and then toss it back down in disgust while grumbling at it. Aaron cut his eyes over to Phillip because he anticipated a flow of profanities to start flying out of Jerry's mouth at any moment.

"How many times do I have to tell that nimrod to leave these damn things together?" he asked to no one in particular while looking for a locking tie down strap that had not been disassembled. "Every time I let the site manager use one of these things he takes it clean apart and then I can't figure out how to put the bastards back together!" he said slamming another one down.

Aaron grinned. He would offer to help, but he knew better. When Jerry was in "a mood," an offer to help would only make the helper become part of the problem.

MEETING AT MATTHEW STREET

"Here. Clip this to the end of the pipe sticking out," he said tossing a red safety flag to Aaron as he continued to rattle around inside the tool box. "Aww right! Here we go," he said extracting a plastic tray which contained a brand new, unused locking strap.

Jerry tossed one end of the strap over to Phillip who hooked it on the passenger side of the truck bed in the rear while Jerry attached the other end on the opposite side and pulled the locking mechanism tightly across the supplies so nothing would come out during the trip home.

"Load up, boys!" Jerry commanded while grabbing the gate of the truck to give it a test pull making sure it was latched well.

Aaron dutifully jumped in the back seat of the dusty king cab while Phillip got in the front. Everything inside was covered in an orange film of red clay dust. In order to get in the back seat, Aaron had to push aside hard hats, gloves, a roll of toilet paper, sweat rags, and bags filled with cheese and peanut butter crackers that Jerry said was a working man's sustenance when he was too busy to stop and eat.

Phillip picked at his index finger and commented, "It's hard to believe that something as small as a splinter could cause so much pain."

Jerry reached into his ashtray and handed him a pair of tweezers that he always kept there.

"Oh! Oh! That reminds me," Aaron said, beating on the center console between the two men sitting in the front seat. "David said you may have had another run-in with your serial killer!" he said to Phillip.

Phillip groaned. This was a difficult subject to talk about. Years before he had been working off and on with a man in the field. They were paired on various taskforces to break up large international sex trafficking rings. The man's name was Mondo Fillingim. He was fairly quiet while they were working, but when he got phone calls it was interesting for Phillip to hear Mondo's side of the conversations. From them Phillip was able to gather that Mondo was some sort of Native American history buff. He would field calls from archeologists asking him where they should go to find historic camp sites along the Escambia River, and once he got an email from the Smithsonian showing him a picture of an item they needed to have identified. He was able to tell them that the artifact was a type of fishing weir once used in Louisiana.

Because of the many locations the twelve had lived over the two millennia, their knowledge of languages was extensive. James, of course, was their best linguist, but Phillip was also very accomplished, which came in handy with the work he did closing the international sex trade operations worldwide. So, when Mondo took a call that sounded like he was speaking Chinese, but it was not the Chinese language Phillip had heard before, he was confused.

"What language was that, Mondo?"

"It was Mikasuki. The medicine man wanted to ask me about some plants from the Old Country."

Good grief! What else did he not know about Mondo? "Where do they speak Mikasuki?"

"Down where the Seminoles are. The Miccosukee are more purists." He thought about it and then clarified, "At least *some* of them are. Some of them are kind of like our version of the Amish. Extremely traditional without electricity and all that stuff because they don't like how *modern* everything has gotten."

"And they're asking you about plants from the old country," he said in amazement. "So, what plants, and where's the old country?"

"Last year I gave them some gopher grass and rabbit tobacco from Pensacola. That and some Yaupon for tea. They use some Snake Root shit for their black drink instead of the real thing. So," he said nonchalantly, "I hook them up with the good stuff every now and then."

Phillip had actually seen Mondo break out his rabbit tobacco while they traveled when he felt a cold coming on. He'd roll the silvery leaves into a tiny ball, light them, and then breathe in the smoke until it smoldered out. It always seemed to help. Mondo would often remain healthy after long international flights when other team members got ill. Knowing how David used herbal remedies throughout the ages, Phillip didn't doubt one bit that this plant was curative. Then Phillip chuckled. How ironic. The other name for rabbit tobacco was "life everlasting."

It was conversations like that which made Phillip realize he might never know the full depth of this quiet, but diverse man. Mondo was amazing for having an uncanny ability to remember facts, people's names and faces. He could see someone many years later and 100 pounds heavier and be able to identify them by the "T" or eyes, nose, and mouth area of their face. He could even identify family groups the same way. Sometimes he recognized a family member belonging to someone on their most wanted listings before they'd even located the actual suspect.

Years before, Phillip and he were working a job out of Cancun when the leader of the sex slavery ring they had been pursuing was found murdered in his penthouse suite. The man had apparently been held captive for days while his killer systematically cut and peeled his skin in small strips. In essence skinning him alive slowly so he would be brought to the brink of death, allowed to recover, and then tortured again later. It was not uncommon for bad guys to meet bad deaths, but this one was particularly gruesome.

Two years later when the same thing happened again in Taipei, Phillip began to research this unusual form of torture to learn more about the origins of it.

It turned out the Red Stick Creek Indians of North America were known to have killed their enemies that way. In fact, one of their killings almost started a war when the Red Sticks captured Tustenuggee Emathla, known as Jim Boy, because he had betrayed the Seminole Indians. When the Seminoles heard that Jim Boy had been captured, they sent word that Jim Boy should be held until they could arrive and have the privilege of killing him. But the Red Sticks got too aggressive while skinning him and he died before the Seminoles could get there. All hell broke loose then. Imagine a feud over someone being tortured to death before they could be tortured to death by someone else! It was an incredible story that Phillip had run across. So, he found the moment when he thought he could casually bring up in his conversation with Mondo the question about Indian tribes and if they had clans.

Mondo replied there were many clans. He himself was from, what he called "a brutal bunch", the Red Stick Creek Indians! He didn't like to talk about them. That was all. He wouldn't say anything more about his heritage nor what about them was "so brutal." But Phillip couldn't help but be nagged by the speculation that they might have their own vigilante working on the taskforce. It was true that many of the worst people they tried to arrest used their own money and connections to get off the hook when caught. Some were almost impossible to shut down. But was Mondo somehow connected to these unique murders?

Shortly after this second incident Mondo almost died while they were working a case. They had just rescued a group of girls from a dilapidated building. They had been held captive in a garage apartment just outside of Atlanta when Mondo came down the flight of rickety wooden steps to leave. Five steps up from the bottom, one of the rotting steps had a slight forward tilt to it and when Mondo lost his balance he was faced with only two options: fall, or jump. He jumped and all of his 311 pounds landed flat footed on the concrete sidewalk below. He appeared to be fine at first, but within an hour, plaque from his heart broke free from a portion of the heart called "the widow maker." Had Phillip not been there to rush him to the hospital, Mondo would have in fact left a widow behind. But he got lucky.

While recovering in the hospital ICU, however, Mondo asked with a scratchy voice, damaged from having a breathing tube inserted the day before, for Phillip to close the door to his room and come to his bedside.

"I want to talk to you," he said patting the edge of his bed asking Phillip to sit next to him. "I'm worried about something," he said almost in a mob boss voice. "I might not make it and I'm a little afraid about some things I've done in life that weren't… that weren't. I don't know how to put it…. Maybe they weren't good things, but they needed to be done. I believe in God and Jesus, but I don't know what God will think of me. What if…?" Mondo fidgeted with the blanket that rested across his chest. "What if I don't make it?"

"Well Mondo," Phillip began. "The only thing I can tell you is what I always found comfort in when I was a young man, and that's the story of King David." Phillip began to count off on his fingers. "He had an affair with someone else's wife. He got her pregnant. And then, he tried to cover things up by having her husband killed in battle. He did! He got him killed. But despite all of that, the Bible says that King David was a man after God's own heart. So, apparently God was able to see past all of his faults and some pretty major sins. God knew that King David had a good heart and was sorry for his shortcomings. Not only did King David get God's forgiveness, but God thought very highly of him. After all of that," he said shaking his head, "we're told that he was a man after God's own heart," Phillip said, looking at Mondo's ashen face. His normally tan skin had lost all its color, an oxygen cannula was in his nose and his lips were still caked with blood where a breathing tube had once been only hours before.

"A man after God's own heart….after all of that?" Mondo said looking down at the foot of his bed at someplace far beyond anything that the eye could see.

With that, the door opened and Mondo's wife came rushing in. She had caught a flight and was seeing Mondo for the first time. Phillip patted Mondo's shoulder and left the hospital.

MEETING AT MATTHEW STREET

That was the last time he saw Mondo. Mondo left their taskforce. Many years passed without any sign of him or further murders until a few months ago. Phillip was working in the Virgin Islands during a torrential downpour brought on by a tropical cyclone. Sheets of rain cascaded down. Phillip and his team were inspecting a small rental house that had been used in the torture of a high profile pedophile they had been pursuing for years. The crime scene was identical to the previous two that Phillip had worked. No finger prints. No hair fibers. No tools left behind. Just a tortured, skinned, dead body handcuffed to a bed.

As Phillip stepped out to the front porch under the protection of a large overhang, the rain came down in a full sheet off the gutterless roof. He took his phone out of his pocket, clicked on contacts and started to type in M-O-N. Mondo's phone number appeared, and he hit send.

Mondo answered immediately, "Hey buddy, you missin' me?"

"I don't know. Where are ya?" Phillip asked.

"I'm around," Mondo said.

Phillip thought for a moment and then asked, "How's your health?"

There was a long pause. "I've got a good heart," Mondo replied, enjoying his double entendre.

Through the rain Phillip squinted and thought he saw the figure of a large man standing on the porch of a house down the street. The blur of the rain ebbed, flowed and shifted in the stiff gusts of wind as he watched the figure run to a parked car, start it and make a U turn in the street heading away from the crime scene.

Phillip heard one last statement from Mondo before the phone went dead. "Hey Phillip... Keep your powder dry."

Lisa Kirkman

CHAPTER TWENTY-ONE

On Monday Stellman got to work at 7:30AM so he could get up with Ron Evans immediately upon his arrival at work. He sat in the lobby area fidgeting until Ron casually entered with his backpack slung over one shoulder. Upon seeing him, Stellman jumped up to meet him. Walking next to Ron, he matched him stride for stride, while he excitedly told him how he'd been successful with his stakeout. They made their way to the elevator while he gave Ron the blow by blow account of how he'd deployed a tracking device on Libby's car and that he needed to know where the car was located. As the elevator doors opened on the 2nd floor they quickly made their way to Ron's office.

Ron enjoyed the technology that they had at their fingertips and was equally excited to see what Stellman had managed to obtain, so upon getting to his office he slung his backpack across his desk and immediately logged onto his computer to pull up the tracking program. At first he was a little rusty at using it, but he repeatedly referenced a collage of sticky notes that were plastered across the wall behind his bank of computer screens and apparently found the notes necessary for him to remember how to successfully retrieve the information.

"Boy!" he said while taking in the information as it came up on his screen. "Talk about paranoid!" Ron said. "Take a look at the route this lady took! She must have known you were on her tail because look, she made a complete loop here," he said pointing at the screen. "And then, over here, she's like right behind the Post Office again on a parallel street going the opposite direction." Ron held his chin in his hand as he viewed the remaining data. "Holy mackerel! Look at this! Another frickin' loop. Man, you messed with her head for sure. You realize that she might not be there anymore, right? If she was *that* in tune to your following her, then she may have bugged out by now. But here it is buddy, that's your address," he said pointing to a stationary flashing dot on the screen. "2752 Matthew Street." Ron leaned back in his chair and crossed his arms. Satisfaction covered his face. Damn, he loved technology!

Stellman jotted down the address on the palm of his hand and made his way to the elevator. He punched the elevator to go to the 4th floor where his office was but not before he hurriedly made his way to his boss's office to give him an update. When he saw that no one was there, he swung by the break room and found his boss standing near the sink stirring a cup of coffee.

Leaning inside the door he announced, "Hey! I have an address on our potential Marcus Cain hijackers," he shared with him.

"You're kidding me! Holy shit, the timing couldn't be better. Hoven just chewed my ass out and said I should start looking for another job if you didn't have something soon. Right now he's got me checking on another person named Marsha or Mara or something. Look… I'm up to my ass in his freakin' alligators. You call Hoven and give him the news about the address and ask him what he wants you to do next. I don't dare make another move without his input and it's still your fucking fault that Cain got away from us to begin with." He tore open and stirred a second package of sugar into his cup. "I don't want to hear his crap anymore about letting him get away, so you handle it. Got it?" he shouted as Stellman eased away from the doorway. "You handle it!"

Damn! Stellman went to his office and checked his contacts for Hoven's number. He was the last person in the world he wanted to talk to and this was not going to go well. He found the number and took a deep breath before dialing. Then he hung up quickly and gave it some further thought about what he'd say.

Practicing his lines he made a few notes on a scratchpad at his desk and then dialed Hoven once again.

"Speak," Hoven answered.

Who answers like that, Stellman wondered? A little rattled, he proceeded "Mr. Hoven, this is Robert Stellman with the…"

"I know who you are, jackass. What do you have for me?" Hoven replied.

"Ahhh… well…sir," Shit this threw him off his game. Pull yourself together Stellman! "Sir, I was able to place a tracking device on one of the suspect's cars and…"

"Excellent! Excellent!" he interrupted. "You may have done better than any interrogation could yield if you've located more than one of the members I'm after," Hoven congratulated.

"Yes sir. Yes. Well, I have an address, sir and we're wanting to know how you'd like us to proceed next, sir," Stellman stumbled over his words feeling like an idiot.

"Give me the address," he replied abruptly.

"2752 Matthew Street, sir," Stellman said referencing the scribble on the palm of his left hand.

MEETING AT MATTHEW STREET

Hilarious laughter erupted on the other end of the phone. Hoven laughed so hard he began to cough. Between coughing and laughing he stopped to take an occasional deep breath before breaking out into laughter again.

"Sir?" Stellman said. But the cackling on the other end of the phone wouldn't stop. "Sir? What did I say?"

"Just a moment," he managed to get out before he continued, "Just a moment. 2752.... 2752 Matthew....Oh my. Let me wipe my eyes." There was a pause. "Oh my.... Ok... that's better. My heavens! Hiding in plain sight. Hahaha. Hiding in plain fucking sight! How stupid! Now I *know* you've found them. It's too much! I can't talk.... Let me call you back with a plan. I just can't talk."

More fading sounds of him laughing could be heard as Hoven took the phone away from his ear and hung up.

What the hell had just happened? Bewildered, Stellman placed the phone back on its receiver and contemplated his next move. He didn't dare tell his boss what had just happened. What if it was something that would get them all in trouble? Why was this so damn hilarious?

Stellman stood up from his desk and paced back and forth in his office trying to decide what his next move might be. He was awaiting a return call from Hoven, but a call concerning what? A hilarious street address? What was funny about that?

He sat back down at his desk and put his head between his hands and tried to think. Who could he turn to? Who? With what? He got up quickly and closed the door to his office before taking out his cell phone. He pressed his home key and verbally commanded, "Call Angela, cell."

"Calling Angela Keene, mobile," replied his phone. Moments later he heard it answer.

"Hello! What's up?" she answered.

"Hey babe. I need your help," he said.

"Sure! What's wrong?" she inquired with concern.

"You know the missing guy?"

"Yes…"

"Well, I had to call the big boss and tell him I found him…"

"Yeees?…"

"And for some reason, he found the address crazy funny? Like, *unusually* so," he explained.

"What's the address? Or can you not tell me?" she inquired, being conscious of the clandestine nature of his job.

"It's 2752 Matthew Street," he said and then paused for her reaction.

The other end of the phone was silent. There was no reaction at all.

"Does that mean anything to you?" he inquired.

"No… nothing. I can't imagine what would be funny about *that*?" she professed.

"2752? Matthew?... Oh! And he said, 'They're hiding in plain sight.' Does that mean *anything* to you?" he asked. He was so grateful to have someone to confide in. He seriously loved this woman.

"Matthew…. Matthew…" she repeated. "I know about three or four guys named Matt, but none of them go by their full name." She gave it more thought, "Honestly, the only thing that comes to mind for me is one of the Gospels. Matthew, Mark, Luke and John," she said.

"That's from the Bible, right?" he asked.

MEETING AT MATTHEW STREET

"Yes. The first four books of the New Testament."

Stellman didn't know anything about the Bible. His parents never took him to church as a child and told him they wanted him to be able to make up his own mind about religion as an adult. But with nothing to compare it to, other than seeing a few people holding Bibles in the air and shouting at his car while he sat at a traffic light, he thought it was a rather distasteful, intrusive organization that was mostly full of rules. Don't drink. Don't dance. Don't whatever.

He became discouraged. Angela's suggestion wasn't a lead at all as far as he was concerned, but he didn't have anything else to go on. "I guess there's no 2752 Matthew Street mentioned in the Bible?" he asked sarcastically.

Angela laughed. "No... No Matthew Streets. But let me pull up my Bible app. I hope I don't hang up on you. I think I can put you on speaker phone and pull up the app at the same time and not disconnect you." There was a pause before she came back and asked in a tinny speaker phone voice, "Tell me the street number again."

"2752," he said.

"OK, Matthew, got that... chapter 27, got it.... verse 52," she said punching the verse up on her app... "Hmmmm. I don't *know*. This says, 'and the tombs broke open. The bodies of many holy people who had died were raised to life.' Gosh! That's interesting. Let me read further back some to get the context of this," she looked at a few verses back from 27:52 to get her bearings and began to read aloud again, skimming over the section in question. 'And when Jesus cried out again in a loud voice, he gave up his spirit (so this would be during his crucifixion)...the curtain of the temple was torn.... earth shook….your verse about the tombs opening…. And the dead people appeared to many.' Huh! I wonder why I never noticed that verse before? That's pretty crazy. Dead people rising from their tombs when Jesus was crucified!" she said with astonishment that she'd not caught that verse in the past when reading the Bible as she had so many times before over the years.

Stellman listened to the ridiculous Bible verse with skepticism until he reflected on what he remembered from the interrogation with Marcus. What was it Marcus had said? The recording was missing, so there was nothing to reference back to. But what was it?... What was it?... Something about dying, seeing people from above, floating, heaven, and then darkness and he saw his dead mother and a dead sibling, I think? Wobbly legs. People were scared of them? It was all a bunch of the delirious ramblings that he sort of ignored at the time Marcus was saying all that weird stuff.

"Thanks babe. Keep thinking about what 2752 Matthew Street might mean and call me if you come up with something. I appreciate your thoughts on all of this," he said before hanging up the line in frustration.

Stellman took out his set of keys from his pocket and opened the top right drawer of his desk. He reached under a stack of papers and took out a crinkled brown paper bag. Opening the nondescript bag, he withdrew a jewelry box, cracked the lid and observed the diamond engagement ring inside. Before he hid it back inside his desk, he made sure the receipt was still in the bag. He'd need to get a refund for his purchase if he got fired.

MEETING AT MATTHEW STREET

CHAPTER TWENTY-TWO

Stellman used satellite imagery to ascertain that the house at 2752 Matthew Street sat by itself at the end of a long private drive surrounded by woods. Oddly enough, there were no other houses on Matthew Street and the property, according to the appraiser's website was located on acreage, and belonged to a foundation.

At the behest of Viktor Hoven, Stellman was to observe the house for any activity or signs of routine comings or goings. Hoven was particularly interested in knowing if it appeared as though twelve people might be staying together in the house.

Stellman was an experienced deer hunter and owned a wide assortment of hunting gear, so at night he set up one of his pop up, camo tent blinds in the woods behind the house and surrounded the base of it using a pair of large clippers with freshly cut limbs and bushes to break up the outline of the tent. This additional real camouflage was enough to fool the eye of anyone who might wander deeper into the property near his blind. He was grateful that the occupants at 2752 Matthew Street didn't appear to own any barking dogs that might give his location away.

After he set up the blind, Stellman eased over to the house and snooped around the trashcans at the side of the garage in hopes of retrieving any type of refuse that might indicate who and how many might be staying inside.

There was evidence of a large amount of trash, but nothing that might be definitive about the inhabitants.

Two days went by and then, he got a huge break. One evening a large man who he had observed often coming and going from the house to a workshop behind the house set up a charcoal grill on the back deck of the house. Stellman was able to count at least seven different people who came and went visiting with the man as he operated the grill. It wasn't until a young woman joined him with a large platter of what appeared to be steaks that Stellman began to strain through the binoculars and try his best to count portions.

As the steaks went on the grill, he was pretty sure he had counted twelve. As they came off at various stages of doneness, he carefully counted them for a second time and came up with twelve again. This would have to be the best proof he could offer Hoven, so he phoned him immediately as dusk fell over his hiding place in the woods.

Hoven advised him that it might be a couple of hours before he could join him, and that he should maintain his position and report back if anyone appeared to leave the premises.

MEETING AT MATTHEW STREET

CHAPTER TWENTY-THREE

While Jerry worked outside on the steaks, Mara surveyed the kitchen and began cleaning up after Jerry. He had made a coleslaw recipe and left pieces of their food processor in various places all around the kitchen. The main unit was on the island. The bowl was next to the oven and the metal disk was next to the sink. Seeing it scattered like that Mara knew it was a sure way to lose an essential part to Libby's prized food processor, rendering the machine virtually useless if not careful, so she gathered the pieces together to wash them.

In the process of washing the metal disk with the various grating features on it, she first hand washed the side Jerry had used with the grating feature. She was careful to run her sponge counter clockwise across the grates so it wouldn't catch on the sponge she was cleaning it with. But when she mindlessly turned it over to clean the other side, she ran her thumb across that side in order to get a firmer grip on the now soapy, slippery disk and accidently slashed a deep gash across her left thumb as it passed over the slicing blade of that side.

"Darn it!" she said, dropping the disk into the sink. She reached for a paper towel to wrap it around her thumb as it began to bleed. When she thought she had successfully stopped the bleeding, she went back to work cleaning the kitchen again, but the gash kept reopening.

Seeing Aaron on his way out to check on Jerry she

stopped him and asked, "Aaron, will you please find me one of those waterproof band aids for this cut I just got?" she requested, holding up her thumb for him to see.

Aaron gladly obliged and hunted through several drawers in the house until he found just the right bandage for her thumb. Returning to the kitchen, he offered to apply the strip for her. As she held out her open palm toward him the long sleeve of her shirt rode slightly up her arm exposing her left wrist. Aaron made an effort to avert his eyes from the visible but faint scars so she wouldn't see that he'd noticed them.

Although her resurrected body came back whole and unblemished, in A.D. 64 Mara almost lost her life for a second time. Just over thirty years had passed since their rising and by this time the group had migrated from Jerusalem to Rome where they lived in the Jewish residential section successfully spreading Christianity in that area when a cataclysmic event took place.

In mid-July of that year, Rome was ablaze when a fire broke out in a shop filled with flammable products. The uncontrollable fire lasted six days and wiped out nearly three quarters of the city. Out of fourteen districts, only four remained intact.

When the fire first broke out, the twelve elect helped hundreds of people escape to fields where they might remain safe from the flames. Then, the ten men of their group returned to help fight the fire alongside the Roman firefighters who had been dispatched. The layout of Rome with narrow winding streets allowed the fire to spread wildly and made efforts to contain it difficult.

On one of the narrow streets, Phillip came upon a small group of their recent Christian converts. They were

MEETING AT MATTHEW STREET

surprisingly intent on stopping the firefighters from making progress. They had blockaded the narrow lane with tables, carts, and every possible item they could lay their hands on to keep the firefighters from being able to pass.

"Ananias! What is going on here?" Phillip asked, perplexed by the actions of his friend and fellow Christian.

"Isn't it wonderful?" Ananias said gleefully sweeping his arm across the hole of the city. "The Lord is returning!"

"No, Ananias. It's a fire. We must extinguish it. Please! Move these things out of our way," Phillip begged.

"No, can't you see it?! It's God's judgement day. The New Kingdom that the Christ spoke of is nigh! We are ready for His judgement! Stand with me!" he beckoned Phillip with excitement before lifting his arms to the heavens to welcome in the approaching flames.

The Roman firefighters and Imperial Soldiers who were fighting the fire alongside Phillip were astounded as they listened to what Ananias was saying. He and a group of his Christian friends were actually welcoming the destruction of their city, not helping, but hindering their attempts to save it. Turning to Phillip to lead the team of firefighters in their next move, Phillip commanded them to press forward and destroy the blockade. When one of the soldiers attacked Ananias to get him out of their way, Ananias fell hard to the ground. He then looked up at Phillip in miffed disbelief. How could his brother in Christ allow these pagan non-believers stop God's will like that? But Phillip pressed on with the others as the passage was opened and their progress continued.

After the fire was contained, many people blamed Emperor Nero for having started the fire for self-serving purposes. Some even reported that he watched from safety and sang happily during the destruction, hoping to rebuild Rome afterward, fresh and new as a modern shrine to himself.

When Nero discovered how much contempt there was toward him, he used the story of the Christians who had blocked the firefighting efforts to cast blame on them instead. He made a huge spectacle of gathering up the Christian believers in Rome and ordered that they be killed in public at Rome's only surviving amphitheater where dogs or lions were enticed to shred their flesh, and to tear limb from limb. After being slaughtered, Nero then ordered that their corpses be used as nighttime torches around the city by being set on fire.

As Nero's men were dispatched to round up more Christians, Mara was waiting in a line to receive supplies that Nero had imported into the community to aid in the relief effort. A group of soldiers approached different people in the line behind her and began asking the locals to point out any known Christians among them. When someone pointed to Ananias, the soldiers approached him and began questioning him.

"I'm not one of them!" he declared nervously as the soldiers surrounded him. He looked around frantically until his eyes fell on Mara, "But that one over there!" he said pointing to her. "She's one of the ones who came to Rome talking about the Christ. I know for a fact that she is one of them!" he said pointing. Other men standing near him who had helped form the barricade with Ananias joined in and energetically confirmed his claims about Mara.

MEETING AT MATTHEW STREET

The soldiers quickly left Ananias, approached Mara and immediately arrested her. She was taken to a prison to await her execution the following day. Due to the relief efforts and the displacement of everyone from their homes, her absence from the group was not noticed and no one was dispatched to find her.

The following day Mara was led out of prison and shackled to a line of seven other prisoners. She was placed at the rear of the group. They were forced to walk a great distance from the prison to the amphitheater so they could be seen by a large number of Rome's citizen along the way. During this trek the group was spat upon, pummeled by stones and debris from the fire, and berated with jeers from the angry, displaced citizens. Every time the person in front of Mara would fall during one of these attacks, the chains connecting them would cause the sharp edges of Mara's shackles to cut deeply into her flesh so that by the time they arrived at the amphitheater, Mara's wrists were raw and bloodied. The smell of the blood running down the prisoner's wrists would only serve to entice the attacking animals all the more by working them into a snarling frenzy as they scrambled to taste more and more of the blood that was already in the air.

The line of prisoners were led into a long breezeway that ran under the stands to the amphitheater. Before the passage opened into the center arena, the guard leading them stopped the group, had them line up against the wall and commanded, "Wait here." Everyone slumped to the ground except Mara.

Emperor Nero would be attending that day's bloodbath, so he was being accompanied by two members of his Praetorian Guard, an elite group from the Imperial

Lisa Kirkman

Roman Army assigned as bodyguards to the emperor. As they prepared for his arrival, one of these elite men began to survey the breezeway leading to the arena. He wanted to make sure it was secure for the Emperor should he need to use it as an escape route in an emergency.

The Praetorian Guard ventured past the line of bedraggled Christians and paid little attention to them since they were shackled. He was more concerned with the others who were gathered further down the breezeway until he noticed one of the prisoners do a double take in his direction.

Looking toward the prisoners with disgust, Lucius gasped and stumbled backward several paces before hitting the wall behind him, knocking the breath out of his lungs. His face went ashen. His heart leapt wildly within his chest. Staring back at him with contempt was Mara, in the flesh, unmistakably alive!

When Lucius was reassigned to Jerusalem by Tiberius, he had received exactly what he wanted in the move, a means to continue his rise up through the military ranks. Now, as a Praetorian Guard, he felt content that this would be the final rank of his career. He was able to enjoy the fineries of the palace, the respect of other soldiers and the Emperor's ear when he needed it. Although he could rise further, he was finally satisfied that he'd achieved his goal in life. But what on earth was happening? What was he seeing before his eyes?

"What are you doing here you worthless piece of skubalon?" Mara spewed at him. "I thought you were wanting your precious assignment to be in Jerusalem!" she said angrily toward Lucius.

If he was not sure before, he knew now that this was she. But how? Lucius rubbed his hands over his eyes to clear them. Was he ill? Was this a hallucination? He pushed himself off the side of the wall and with great hesitation made his way toward Mara walking sideways so his feet would be prepared to spring away from whatever this was before him. His eyes bulged with fear, his shoulders were hunched like a scared animal as he approached her tentatively and raised one finger to poke her shoulder. His illusion had mass!

"Have you come to see me die once more?" she asked with venom.

"This can't be happening. It's not possible. I returned you to Jerusalem like Tiberius said to. I gave you over for a Jewish burial," he said.

"And now you can hand me over for a Christian burial," she said sarcastically.

Lucius didn't hesitate. He looked to the front of the line of prisoners. "Guard! Guard! Come here!" he said motioning toward Mara. "Release her!"

The guard looked at Lucius's rank and without delay, did as he was told. Once Mara's restraints were undone Lucius stepped back and surveyed her from head to toe, but Mara came at him aggressively and thrust both of her arms out at Lucius, ramming him in the shoulders knocking him backward several steps while saying, "They raped me!" She proceeded toward him again as he stumbled backward. Again, she pushed him with even greater force using every thrust at his shoulders to emphasize each of her punctuated words. "Again and again!" she said with fury in her eyes.

Lucius's back was pressed against the stone wall of the breezeway as Mara rammed her forearm firmly against his neck causing him to choke. Seeing this, she felt the sweet sense of revenge run through her veins. She let up slightly before thrusting her arm against his neck again, enjoying the sight of his squirming under *her* control. Lucius remained frozen in disbelief. How could he fight a ghost who had come back to haunt and condemn him?

Mara stepped back, looking at the cowering man standing before her. Lucius saw the pure hate in her eyes as her disdain for him seared deep into his core. Without a word, she turned toward the exit and began to walk away.

Lucius didn't move a muscle and remained with his back against the wall, he only turned his head in her direction to see her leaving. Her body was merely a silhouette against the light at the end of the darkened tunnel. As she walked, however, he noticed that her gait appeared to be unusual. Her legs were spread further apart than normal and as his eyes adjusted he was able to make out her blood stained robes. She had been raped and brutally sodomized while in prison, to the point of hemorrhaging.

"I'm sorry!" he shouted as his heart broke for her for a second time in his life.

Mara kept walking without breaking stride.

"Forgive me!" he pleaded.

Mara stopped walking and stood still in her tracks. She knew what she was supposed to do as a Christian. But again she continued on her path toward the exit.

"Please!" Lucius cried out in guttural anguish as he fell to his knees.

Mara stopped again, inhaled deeply while looking skyward at the dark grey, arched ceiling over her head. Then she let her chin drop to her chest with a bounce. Shaking her head in disbelief she asked herself why God would want her to *ever* forgive this man. Slowly, she turned around and looked at the tear stained face looking back at her. For what seemed like an eternity to Lucius, she just stared at his brokenness before she finally admitted, "I need assistance getting home. I'm badly hurt," she said.

Lucius sprang up and yelled over his shoulder to the guard, "Tell the other Praetorian there was an emergency that I had to attend to!" He then ran to Mara and swept her from her feet. Cradling her, he carried her in his arms to where the others were known to be camping while helping with the relief efforts in Rome.

The entire way Lucius cried tears of joy. He kissed the top of Mara's head repeatedly and thanked her profusely for extending her forgiveness toward him. For the first time in 30 years he felt the heavy burden of his past lifted from his chest. He was overcome with relief!

◆◆◆

Four years later in A.D. 68, a new Emperor was put in place in Rome. An edict was sent out that Nero should be found, returned and executed. Before that could happen, Nero decided to take his own life. Repeatedly, he tried to commit suicide, but found it too difficult to accomplish. It's said that he asked his aid to help him end his life so he would not have to face a more brutal end at the hands of Emperor Galba.

A rumor went around that Nero didn't actually commit suicide, as some accounts claimed. Another rumor circulated that someone of his likeness was seen working with a man named Lucius as the two established a Christian ministry in Asia.

But that was just a rumor.

◆◆◆

Scars. They can be physical or mental. Aaron made sure the bandage on Mara's thumb was not fastened too tightly before giving it a tiny kiss and saying tenderly with a gentle smile… "All better."

MEETING AT MATTHEW STREET

CHAPTER TWENTY-FOUR

The residents at 2752 Matthew Street enjoyed another meal that Libby didn't have to cook before retiring to the meeting room where they once again took up the matter of their future.

James opened the meeting and it was obvious by the look on his face that he had struggled greatly with what he was about to share with the group.

"As you know," he began, "Marcus mentioned that he was visited while he was being held for interrogation by a man who identified Marcus as being 'one of twelve.' Well, Simon and I have not shared something with you," he said while curious, surprised looks were shared among all the members of the group. "Ninety years ago Simon witnessed a disturbing scene while visiting the Vatican when he was working on some research for one of his books. He saw a pregnant woman who had escaped from an apparent exorcism. She spoke to him in a demonic voice." Worried looks turned toward Simon who was biting his lower lip while staring at his feet with his head bowed, slightly nodding yes. James continued, "She said, 'You've met your match One of Twelve'."

There were audible gasps.

"Oh, my gosh! You're kidding me," Libby exclaimed.

"Why didn't you tell us? Phillip asked.

"I have chills," said Mara running her hands up her arms.

James continued, "I'm concerned about what this could mean. The man who used the same phrase with Marcus during his interrogation (could be coincidence, maybe not) appeared to be close to ninety years of age and Simon's encounter was...." James paused while everyone considered the implications.

"Ninety years ago," Andrew finished the sentence while the room fell silent for a few moments.

"Regardless of what any of this means, it appears that *someone* is aware of our presence and that leads me to my next revelation, and I'm sorry, I don't mean that as a pun using the word 'revelation,' because I need you to know that I met with John, the writer of Revelation on the Island of Patmos in regard to our mission as a group. I got to see him because a sympathizer to the cause of Christianity, a guard who John had converted during his imprisonment there, sneaked me in to meet with him.

He warned me that when Jesus's twelve disciples drew lots and separated from one another to evangelize around the world, they left each other vulnerable to attack. He said that this was why so many had been martyred except, so far, for himself. John was quite clear that he had had a vision that included us. He advised that we should remain united as a group until the time mentioned in Isaiah 5:20." James walked over and stood behind their ancient, prized pedestal upon which the large Bible rested and placed a ribbon to mark the page in Matthew before he turned to Isaiah 5:20 and read the following.

"Woe to those who call evil good, and good evil; Who substitute darkness for light and light for darkness; Who substitute bitter for sweet and sweet for bitter." James returned the Bible to the page they always left it on in the book of Matthew.

"John told me that a time would come when the world would seem to be upside down. Right and just things would be looked upon as wrong. Goodness would be looked upon as bad. Evil things would be revered as good."

Phillip considered the powerful, wealthy men who were profiting from, and gladly networking with pedophiles.

Libby thought of rampant drug abuse and the legalization of such. Or the outrage some had over seeing dogs being held in cold cages while the right to have an abortion received a standing ovation by law makers in her own state. She thought of late term, partial birth abortions where babies would be delivered from their feet to their neck, kicking in the arms of the doctor before having their skulls punctured by scissors so the brain could be suctioned out and the skull collapsed for the final delivery of their now lifeless bodies. Who would clap for something as serious as that? Surely the people who made the grave decision to abort didn't go into it rejoicefully clapping over the struggle they had been faced with while dealing with their unwanted pregnancy. A dog's rights being placed over termination of a viable third trimester human. Couldn't anyone see how upside down that thinking was? Honestly! Think about it. The same people who applauded the right to kill a human baby found outrage over elephants performing in circuses, dogs being left outside in the winter, and they even took a case to court requesting that chimpanzees have the same rights as people?

Lisa Kirkman

Andrew recalled a coworker coming to him distraught because he had been asked to create problems for organizations that appeared to be upstanding entities.

Aaron knew this verse far too well and witnessed it firsthand more than any of the others in their group. He thought of the young men he worked with who wanted to become gang members who actually considered murdering someone in order to pass initiation and become a member of a particular gang. They considered murder a positive thing that elevated their status.

One boy, with a football scholarship, borrowed money from an exceptional woman at his church to pay off a gang debt. When she demanded he work to repay her, he murdered her late one night, in her home, using a gun he had stolen from his girlfriend. Such potential wasted! Such a wonderful woman killed simply because she showed concern and kindness toward a young man she wanted to help.

Aaron also thought about the new directive he had received from the schoolboard. He was required to give a D on all math tests just for showing up for the test, regardless if the test was taken by the student or not. Furthermore, he was told that missed due dates for assignments should no longer result in the lowering of a grade. It was absurd what he saw happening in education.

One of his favorite students broke his heart recently. She had overcome such great adversity. She had been raised by her grandmother after her own mother and the man she assumed was her father both died of aids. In her early years she was prostituted out by her own mother for drug money. Her younger brother was born with a heart defect and an addiction to drugs.

MEETING AT MATTHEW STREET

She had everything going against her except for a desire to run! Run away from the life she had. So, she excelled at track, did all her class assignments, and had a determination like no one he had ever met in his extended life. She had a mission and that mission was to earn a scholarship and escape the life she had been dealt. She had been able to compartmentalize the past as not having been of her own doing. But her future? Her future was squarely going to be in her own control.

Aaron had no doubt that she'd achieve this goal until a senior at her high school who also wished to get a scholarship decided to falsely claim that he wished to be reclassified as a female when he realized his abilities were just shy of what the universities were awarding scholarships for. He was desperate too. He wanted out of his own family circumstances and decided to use any means available to him to escape his neighborhood and the gangs who had targeted him. Who was at fault here? Could Aaron blame the boy for his own desperation? Both of them were survivors. Both were determined.

When the imposter of gender reassignment was awarded the scholarship Aaron's prize student lost, the twelve stepped forward and made her dream possible by creating a fund for her use for as long as she might continue her education and the path that would allow her to escape from the life that kept beating her backwards.

All the lines of right and wrong were intentionally being blurred. But for what purpose? So wrong could be called good enough, or that good really didn't matter and wasn't necessary? Was it to cause confusion? To destroy a strong nation by weakening its youth and destroying it from the bottom up?

James continued, "I have to admit, I heard someone using that verse on a radio program probably back in the 1990's and I couldn't see it back then. But every year since, I've said to myself repeatedly, 'Woe to those who call good evil, and evil good' and I've thought about what John said we should do when that time comes." James looked at the group as all eyes were trained on him for the instruction that had come from John of Patmos, the writer of the book of Revelation, the person to whom God revealed visions of the end times.

"John said that we should never tell people who we are because we would surely risk being worshipped unjustly and that would distract from our mission, potentially causing us to stumble by putting our own egos in front of God's purpose. But he said a day would come when a mighty nation, which had been formed by people professing a faith in God, would begin to crumble. When good things are called bad and bad things are called good...and that's when we should divulge our true identities."

The noise in the room rose as everyone began to talk about how diametrically opposed that was to everything they'd ever done as a group. Imagine the chaos! Disbelief by the public. Push back from Christian churches, as well as non-Christian faiths. Harassment by the media. Claims of heresy. Like the early apostles, they would be murdered figuratively or even more likely, literally for going against the current philosophy. In a world where the truth was being presented as a lie, there was no way that they could come forward *now*! No one would be made happy by their revelation to the world. Impossible! It would be horrific!

MEETING AT MATTHEW STREET

"Granted, it would be a huge change for us. We'd need to decide just how we'd go about doing it. I'm assuming we'd do it a little along the way? Or trust in God that He will divulge a plan to us as we go? It's something to be discussed, certainly. I wouldn't jump into it quickly by any means," he concluded while everyone talked amongst themselves, dumbfounded by all the news they'd just received.

Meanwhile, Robert Stellman was meeting Viktor Hoven a block from 2752 Matthew Street to go over their strategy for raiding the premises. Stellman was shocked when Hoven arrived without any backup. How was he intending to storm a place with as many as twelve people inside without additional help?

"Mr. Hoven, may I ask who these people are to you?" Stellman inquired.

"They are disrupters. They have interfered with my work all my life and I need them eliminated," he said.

Stellman wasn't sure what he meant by "eliminated." Did he want their foundation closed down? Surely he didn't mean *eliminate* as in killed? These people didn't look old enough to have disrupted a 90 year old man's *entire* life. They must be part of an organization. But an organization of twelve people? It was confusing and he had more questions than he had answers.

Stellman had done some additional research into Viktor Hoven's life, over the past few days. If anyone was disrupting things, it looked more like Hoven was doing that sort of mischief. He provided printed signs to protestors, outfitted them with masks, and even bussed protestors-for-hire into areas where he wanted to plant demonstrators and unrest. As someone with years of law enforcement background, Stellman didn't like the tactics his boss was reported to have used to get his way.

"Let's go to their back door first and see if it's unlocked." Hoven suggested, "I'd rather come in quietly and hope to catch them off guard than to storm in and have them scatter."

"You're the boss," Stellman said, unsure that this aging man was executing the best plan possible, but this was Hoven's raid and he was there primarily to save his job with the agency.

Stellman was grateful for the moonlight of a nearly full moon as he led Hoven around the garage and along the rear wall of the house toward the back door. It was the door he'd seen the larger man exiting out of when he was going to and from the workshop located behind the house. Upon reaching the door, Stellman gave the door handle a gentle twist and the door gave a slight pop as the latch disengaged from the mortise plate. Stellman motioned to Hoven that they could enter.

When Stellman opened the door, Hoven extracted a Russian Kalashnikov from his jacket, made a quarter turn away from Stellman and jacked a round into the chamber of the pistol before proceeding inside. Stellman withdrew his Glock and followed him.

As they made their way stealthily down the back hallway, voices could be heard in a room off to their right. They eased closer to the entrance of the room where the twelve were gathered, discussing what James had just revealed to them. Before Stellman knew what was happening, Hoven sprang around the corner to the room and shouted, "No one move!" To emphasize the seriousness of his command, Hoven aimed for a vase sitting next to David and shot it. A shard flew off the shattered vase and hit David in the arm cutting him deeply. David jumped up gripped his arm tightly to stop the bleeding.

Stellman's ears were ringing from the unexpected gunshot as he moved in behind Hoven and saw the shocked looks on all the faces before him.

Waving his pistol at the group, Hoven commanded everyone to move toward one corner of the room next to the fireplace. As they complied Marcus said under his breath, "That's the man I told you about." This news compounded their fear as they moved into place per Hoven's instructions. But as Mara passed Hoven to join the others, he grabbed her aggressively by the arm and forced her back down onto a nearby chair, "Not you," he said.

"Stellman, get over there and keep your gun on them," he commanded. He looked on the huddled group with contempt as the men sheltered Libby behind them, "No quick movements or you'll be shot!" he warned.

When Hoven turned around to look at Mara recoiled next to him, he seemed to become distracted suddenly by what he saw on the walls directly behind her. There, surrounding Mara's piano were exquisite paintings of angels, Jesus, the Virgin Mary and other paintings depicting children in prayer with beams of light shining down on them from above. Hoven's expression changed on his face. It turned red with fury. He reached into his pocket and extracted a switchblade which he expertly opened with a flick of his wrist. In a rage he approached the painting of Jesus and started slashing at it over and over again, tearing it to shreds.

When he'd destroyed the work of art he turned around and saw the sheet music resting on the piano's music rack. The title read, "How Great Thou Art." It appeared to infuriate him even more, so he took his arm and like a bulldozer swept all the photos off the top of Mara's piano sending them crashing to the floor. Then, taking a nearby bronze sculpture he used it like a sledgehammer. With super human strength he beat the top of the piano, causing a cacophony of sound to emit from the strings within as the lid turned into a blast of splinters.

Stellman watched in stunned amazement as this madman continued with his tantrum, picking up priceless relics from around the room and smashing them to bits. As he did this Marcus lunged for the podium in an effort to shield it from Hoven's tirade but Stellman blocked the move like a linebacker, sending him hard to the floor at his feet. Marcus reached up toward Stellman with a pleading hand and begged, "Please save our podium. It's the one thing we don't want to lose."

Stellman looked to his left and saw that in blocking Marcus's lunge, he had braced himself with one hand on top of the podium Marcus was trying to protect. Under his hand lay a large book. He looked at the opened page and saw written across the top on the left page Matthew 26:70. Looking at the right hand page he read the heading at the top of that page. It read Matthew 27:57. He looked down at Marcus's pleading face and then flipped the book over to read what was on the front cover. Holy Bible.

Having destroyed much of the room, Hoven turned his attention to Mara and approaching her, whipped his pistol across her face. Upon seeing that, Aaron flew forward out of the corner of the room and lunged at

MEETING AT MATTHEW STREET

Hoven, but Hoven raised his pistol and shot at Aaron. The bullet grazed his forehead, knocking him out and sending him to the ground as a pool of blood quickly formed under his head.

Mara leapt to her feet and threw herself across Aaron screaming, "No!! Aaron! No!!!"

Hoven reached down and yanked her to her feet by the back of her shirt before grasping her tightly from behind. With her body pressed close to his, his wet lips murmured into her ear, "You've met your match, one of twelve." He used the tip of his gun in his right hand to push Mara's face closer to his own as he ran his tongue up the side of her cheek and promised her, "Don't worry. You'll be spared. *So* pretty!" he whispered. "And your beauty can *never* fade over time. I'll be able to sell you over and over again to heads of state like Tiberius. All the most debase perverts of the world will have their way with you from here until eternity. I'm so glad you're immortal. You will be my favorite toy to play with and the people I sell you to will probably even let me watch if I'm lucky!" he bit her neck and she cried out in pain.

At the sound of her scream, Aaron came to and staggered to his feet. Still quite dazed, he lunged again for Hoven and knocked the gun from his hand. As they struggled, Hoven yelled to Stellman, "Shoot him! Shoot him!"

Stellman raised his Glock and took careful aim at the two struggling men, time slowed down and he witnessed everything before him taking place in slow motion. Just as he squeezed the trigger, Phillip barreled toward Stellman in an effort to tackle him, but it was too late. The carefully aimed bullet had left its chamber and successfully hit its target.

CHAPTER TWENTY-FIVE

When the ambulance arrived at the ER the staff went to work evaluating the comatose patient for signs of brainstem function. A CT scan was ordered to check for signs of an intracranial hematoma. Pupils were checked for a response to light, and a Glasgow Coma Scale or GCS was noted as being only a 5.

Due to their initial findings, surgical treatment was deemed unwarranted. The patient would not survive the perforating wound to his left frontal lobe. He was placed in one of the spare ER rooms for the few hours it might take for the heart to realize that the brain was dead.

MEETING AT MATTHEW STREET

CHAPTER TWENTY-SIX

Robert Stellman looked at his reflection in the mirror and adjusted his tie before turning to his best man and asking with a huge grin, "How do I look?"

With the kindness of a father he replied, "You look as happy as I was when I got married."

Stellman reached out to shake his best man's hand but pulled him close and hugged him while slapping him on the back saying, "Thanks for agreeing to be my best man."

"Oh no. I'm honored...quite honored. But remember, Best Man today, Boss Man when you return from your honeymoon."

"You got it boss," Stellman agreed as the two men made their way to the chapel foyer to greet guests as they arrived for the wedding.

Beyond the closed double doors to the small wedding chapel Angela Keene was sitting on the front row bench. She was dressed in a wedding gown with her eyes closed and head bowed in deep prayer.

Quietly, so as not to disturb her, the last few flowers were attached to the pew ends behind Angela.

When Angela finish her prayer, she raised her head, looked behind her and exclaimed, "How lovely! Those are the most beautiful arrangements I've ever seen! You're so talented," she praised.

"Were you praying about your marriage?"

"Yes," Angela said as Libby sat down beside her and patted her on the leg.

"Don't worry. It takes work, but Robert will be your very best friend. There's nothing like having a spouse who's your friend to share your life with," she reminisced. "When you get back from your honeymoon I'm going to tell you all about my deceased husband and about some very unique experiences I've had that might surprise you. But right now, you need to get back to the dressing room before your guests arrive. And make sure Robert doesn't see you! It's bad luck."

As Angela walked up the aisle, James passed her and went toward Libby. He was always so handsome in his suits. Libby reached up and brushed off one of his shoulders.

"Libby?" James said.

"James?" She replied.

"Would you like to go to dinner and a movie with me this week?"

She laughed, "That almost sounded like an invitation to a date!"

"What if it was?" James asked.

Startled, Libby became flustered. They had always had a rule not to date one another, but it appeared that they were entering a whole new era. Butterflies tickled her insides and she felt more alive than she had in centuries.

Taking him by his arm, she made James step to one side slightly as a few guests began to arrive in the chapel.

"I hope you know I'm older than you," she warned playfully.

"What? Are you worried you'll die before I do?" He laughed.

"I guess not."

MEETING AT MATTHEW STREET

"You guess not about going on the date.... or....?"

"Oh no. It's most certainly...oh, yes, a date. Yes! How exciting! I'm ...I'm flattered beyond words," she said, happily sliding her arm through the crook of James's and rubbing his bicep as he led her to her seat. "A date!" she said again and smiled.

He leaned his head in close to hers, "If we shouldn't call good evil, then I shouldn't deny all the good I've admire in you all these years," he said while taking her hand and ushering her to the groom's side of the chapel.

"Oh no. I'm sitting on the bride's side," she corrected. "I've decided to share my identity with Angela," she said looking up into James's eyes seeking a response.

He nodded in approval and said, "Good choice. I'll be back in a moment after I speak with the limo driver."

As she sat down next to a friend of the bride's, she exclaimed like a schoolgirl, "I'm Libby, nice to meet you." She turned away, but suddenly turned back and blurted, "I've just been asked out on a date!"

The strangers next to her smiled at the unexpected comment. The woman laughed and said, "Well, congratulations," before she turned to her husband and squeezed his hand.

The wedding was officiated by Simon. Mara was one of the bridesmaids and Aaron was a groomsman, sporting a gauze bandage on his left temple where Hoven had grazed him. Stellman's new boss, Marcus, was his best man.

As the wedding party gathered for photos, David, the man who refused to have pictures made of himself insisted on numerous group photos and after he had posed for the final one, they all recessed up the chapel aisle.

Thinking about Aaron's brush with death, Andrew turned to David and asked, "Doc, what are the odds that none of us would have been killed in 2000 years?"

With a shrug of his shoulders David said, "What are the odds we'd be resurrected from the dead in the first place?" he responded, with a sly grin.

Overhearing the conversation, Peter looked over his shoulder and responded, "One in one billion."

"Leave it to the numbers guy to know the answer!" Andrew said, slapping Peter on the back.

Bringing up the rear Mara took her bridesmaid bouquet and playfully touched it against the tip of Aaron's nose. Then she said, "Oh no. I think I got some pollen on your face. Here...let me help you," she said while stopping Aaron and facing him. She brushed the imaginary pollen from the tip of his nose and then gently touched the bandage at the side of his temple.

"Does it hurt?" She asked, drawing closer to him as if to get a better look.

"It's fine," he said gazing down into her eyes.

"I'd like to kiss it and make it better," she said softly as she stroked his face.

Breathing in the scent of her perfume Aaron closed his eyes briefly and reopened them almost in disbelief over the moment. It was the moment he'd always longed for. Then he gently, and respectfully offered his lips to hers.

Aaron and Mara walked out hand in hand. She had suffered tragically, but he vowed to be there for her as a gentle companion who, in her own time, would show her what true love really was.

Later that evening Libby sat at the large dining room table as Simon handed a thick stack of papers to her. She pounded the stack on all four sides to make sure all the pages were flush before clipping them together with an oversized binder clip.

Mara and Aaron walked in. "What are we working on?" Mara asked.

"It's Simon's latest book and it's about us!" Libby explained. "It's called Meeting at Matthew Street."

"Oh, a non-fiction book, eh?" Aaron said.

"Yes, and now that this book is complete Simon better get ready to become *my* proof reader for a while!" Libby announced.

"I'm all in with helping you three with your book," Simon responded.

"You three? What's going on?" Mara asked.

"Amos, Jerry and I are writing a cookbook of our favorite recipes," she said puffing up her chest with a hint of cockiness.

"That's awesome!" Mara exclaimed. "I want a first edition autographed copy."

"What will it be called?" Aaron asked.

"Our working title is Time Tested Recipes Resurrected… at least that's the title for now." Libby said with a flick of her hair at Mara and Aaron, in an unabashed display of pleasure in herself and the exciting new endeavor on her horizon.

She ended with a "so there" nod toward them before Libby appeared to look concerned while canvasing the tabletop for something that was missing, "Where's the title page to your book, Simon?"

"Well, I was wondering," he said taking a seat at the large table where Libby and the others sat. "Should I use my real name or a pseudonym this time?" he asked those gathered in the room.

Lisa Kirkman

Aaron and Mara quickly took a seat with the others in excitement. This was a game they often played, coming up with the latest pseudonym for Simon's books. Normally it was the first name of one of their acquaintances and the last name of another. Once they used the actual name of a preacher they knew. He received several calls for interviews about the commentary everyone assumed he had penned.

"I'm sort of on the fence about it," Simon said.

"How about Robert Keene?" Phillip suggested, using Stellman and Angela's names.

"You could use your own name now, Simon," David suggested, since they had decided that it was time to reveal their true identities.

Giving David's suggestion some thought, Libby warned, "You know Simon, the book will be considered quite controversial. It'll bring a lot of attention on you and you'd have to deal with the public. Would you be comfortable with that?" she asked, knowing that he would not. Simon was not the people person that some of them were. He preferred working in his study with a book as his companion.

David laughed. "Aw, I just had a funny thought when you said that about being uncomfortable with the public." He laughed again. "I don't know if you remember the lady I mentioned who had run a business from her home for 30 years? But what if you use *her* name? That would be funny. It might get her out of the house some. Maybe you could get her to take the book out on book tours and to tradeshows. All that stuff?" David suggested. "If we're each telling someone who we are, she can be 'my someone,' " David offered.

MEETING AT MATTHEW STREET

Simon slid a piece of paper across the dining room table toward David and tapped on top of it. "Write her name down for me." After getting it back from David, he went to his computer in the other room. Moments later he returned with a sheet of paper and handed Libby the cover sheet to his manuscript with the name that David suggested as the author of their newest book, Meeting at Matthew Street.

CHAPTER TWENTY-SEVEN

Viktor Hoven's mortally wounded body lay in the emergency room while nurses watched the monitor in the next room so a "time of death" could be officially called at any moment. When it appeared that death was not imminent, he was moved to a remote room in the ICU. Again, it was considered just a matter of time before his heart would realize that the rest of the body had already died. The live feed video monitor in his room would occasionally show his body jerk with a sudden twitch. No one took much notice of these movements. It was common to see as the body went through the final stages of death. For that matter, it was even possible for a body to continue to move post-mortem for more than a year as ligaments went through various stages of drying. The morgue staff, however, never could get used to the occasional body that would sit bolt upright on the autopsy table. No matter how immune to the experiences and gruesomeness of death they might be, this one phenomenon "creeped out" even the most senior technicians.

So, when Hoven's heart monitor finally flat lined weeks after the shooting, the head nurse casually reached over and flipped the switch to kill the sound. Then she paged the attending doctor to come make the time of death call to be noted on the death certificate.

When Dr. Rogers finished with the patient he was attending to on the other side of the ICU, he stopped by the nurse's station to pick up Hoven's medical chart, and death record paperwork, before making his way to Hoven's bedside for the obligatory final assessment.

Carrying the Hoven chart in his left hand and making a recorded note on his digital recorder with his right, he didn't even look up until he'd finished recording his instructions concerning the last patient he'd seen. He was standing in the doorway when he looked up and saw a room with an empty bed in it. Feeling rather stupid for having entered the wrong ICU room, he took 3 steps backward and looked at the placard just outside the door. It read Room 9. This was the correct room. He then flipped through the chart to see if another physician had called the time of death and that perhaps Hoven's body had already been taken to the morgue. They must have needed the bed pretty urgently to have managed to have all of that take place so quickly. He'd only just received the page to come call the time of death.

Dr. Rogers returned to the nurse's station and handed the chart to the head nurse and asked, "Who called the Hoven death?"

The nurse looked at him confused and said, "No one. We were waiting for you."

"Well, I can't exactly make an official call without a body. Was the morgue called already?"

"No. Of course not. Anyway, they'd take forever to get here," she responded, now becoming as confused as the doctor was. Not trusting him to be pulling a practical joke on her, she got up and went to Room 9 in the far corner of the ICU ward and looked in. She immediately turned around and placed her hands on her hips in confusion and looked all around the ICU to see who was within her sight, but everyone was busy tending to patients in various rooms throughout the ward.

Lisa Kirkman

She then returned with Dr. Rogers to her bank of monitors at the nurse's station and ran Room 9's monitor backwards by about 15 minutes until she saw Hoven on the gurney in his room. With Dr. Rogers intently looking over her shoulder, they watched the last few minutes of footage and saw Hoven, undulating wildly, as his body went into convulsions before coming to a complete rest. This was not unexpected, they assumed this was simply his death throws prior to the monitor flat lining. Instead, Hoven reached across his chest and pulled all the lead lines off of his body causing the equipment to sound off. He sat bolt upright on the gurney, looked around the room briefly and was seen getting out of bed, leaving the visual field of the room monitors.

Further review of Hospital cameras showed Hoven leaving the ICU ward and wandering into random rooms where other patients were recovering from surgery. Apparently, he was looking for a set of street clothes he might be able to change into. After several failed attempts, he was finally seen, dressed and leaving the hospital before camera footage lost sight of his departure.

By 6 P.M. that evening the local news carried the video footage of the mortally wounded man rising from his ICU gurney and wandering off. By 10 P.M. it was on all the cable news stations and by the next day it was trending on YouTube and had been seen by millions worldwide.

Hours before the news crews had a chance to converge on the hospital media department for comments, Stellman's cell phone rang. It was a call from a friend of his who worked security at the hospital. He was phoning him to share the odd news about Hoven's miraculous recovery and disappearance.

MEETING AT MATTHEW STREET

Within minutes of the call, the residents of 2752 Matthew Street were informed and they quickly began the process of abandoning their safe house. Mara brought down a box of her most prized pigments and brushes for painting. Jerry looked out back for some old hand tools he particularly cherished, not for use, but for the memory of having used them in his past. David filled trashcans full of the perishable foods so the refrigerator could be unplugged and left ajar. Simon loaded up his computer and a few rare books he was currently using for research. Amos gathered random items from the kitchen and when he came to the drawer of mismatched trivets, he lovingly placed them into the box he was filling.

As the house became ghostly quiet, James found Libby in the meeting room gathering everyone's diaries from under her side table. No words were exchanged between them as their eyes met. A knowing glance said it all.

James went to the podium and got ready to close the Bible. Instead of being opened to Matthew 27, the Bible was opened to Revelation 13. Curiously, he began to scan the passage.

"And rising from the sea was a beast with ten horns." Could those be the ten nations that Hoven had control over, James wondered? "And seven heads." Hoven had six sons working with him. "The beast was like a leopard with feet like a bear's," James considered the age spots on Hoven's face. "And a mouth like a lion," with his wet, liver-looking lips. "And the beast was given great power, a throne and authority. One of the beast's heads appeared to be slain to death, and when the wound healed, the whole earth marveled after the beast and worshipped the beast, asking, 'Who is like the beast or able to make war against it?' "

James closed the Bible and handed it to David who had entered the room to simply say, "It's time."

James picked up the podium and followed Libby and David to Jerry's pickup truck parked out front, facing forward, ready to depart. All the others had left and were safely on their way. The rear seat of the king cab was surprisingly empty, save for the red clay construction dust on the now visible floor mats. David helped Libby inside the back with her stack of diaries before climbing in the front passenger seat.

The bed of Jerry's pickup was only modestly filled. When one's life is reduced to what can be carried easily, it's surprising to know just how little "things" matter. Mismatched trivets and useless hand tools take on a value that surpasses all the king's gold.

When James handed the podium off to Jerry, he opened the bed of the truck to reveal a finely crafted wooden crate lined in a handmade quilt. The podium was gently lowered into the box before being covered by the quilt and the lid softly closed.

As Jerry faced James at the rear of the truck, James extended his hand to Jerry and shook it saying, "Thank you Jerry. This has been a fine home you crafted for us. One hundred years in one location. Amazing! We've all enjoyed the stability it gave us. I can honestly say that it will always be the one place we'll all remember as 'home'."

Jerry hung his head and James saw a quiver pass across his firm jawline. The two men embraced before taking one last look at 2752 Matthew Street.

MEETING AT MATTHEW STREET

As they drove away, Libby didn't cry as she thought she might. Instead she said a prayer of thanks for the extended time God had granted them to remain in one place as long as He had. Then, in her heart she sang, "Praise God from Whom all blessings flow. Praise Him all creatures here below. Praise Him above the heavenly host. Praise Father, Son and Holy Ghost." They were safe. "Amen."

As Jerry's truck exited the area one last time, the podium inside the wooden crate lay safely bundled within Mara's quilt. To the unknowing eye the quilt was grotesque. The fabrics were soiled, tattered, and disintegrating in many areas. Patches of fabrics from various locations around the globe were incorporated into the piece. It had been patched and re-patched time and time again using newer and newer materials as the quilt aged. But faintly in the middle could be seen the faded shape of a brown cross. And, if you looked closely, draped over the arms of the cross was one of the most soiled and tattered patches of all. Wear, blood, dirt and years had long since stripped it of its original beautiful color. But Mara remembered its purple color well.

Back in the kitchen on the island lay a note for Hoven to find. It was written in Koine Greek. It read, "Blessed are the praus, for they shall inherit the earth. We are unsheathing our weapons." It was signed by the twelve, but interestingly, added to the list were some new names. New recruits, so to speak. They were: Robert Stellman, Angela Stellman, Lisa Kirkman, Phil Kittell, Stephen Zieman, Janice Floyd, Tom Barthel, Charles Pickering, Jill Grove, Glenn Miller, Chaplain Bryan Crittendon, and James Billie.

Lisa Kirkman

When Hoven saw the message, his heart skipped a beat. The secret was no longer a secret and his own identity would now be known! He knew that as new recruits brought in addition warriors for the cause, the exponential ramifications were unfathomable. As the realization struck him, it caused a shiver to go up Hoven's ruthless spine.

The twelve were no longer twelve because, "Who is able to make war against the beast?" The elect will make war against the beast. And if you are reading these words, then you have also been chosen to join the fight. You have been selected to go forward from this day onward with the following admonition. In your days ahead, do not let the beast deceive you by calling evil good and good evil. Do not put darkness in the place of light or light for darkness. Do not put bitter for sweet and sweet for bitter. And remember what is known by the former residents of 2752 Matthew Street. There IS a God and you have been called out by Him to declare to the world…I AM PRAUS!

Meeting adjourned.

MEETING AT MATTHEW STREET

Coming Soon!
TIME TESTED RECIPES RESURRECTED
Here's a taste of what's to come!

RECIPES

LIBBY'S SAUSAGE CORNBREAD

Preheat oven to 375 ºF.
- 1/2 pound Conecuh Sausage (or smoked sausage links), sliced and browned
- 4 eggs
- 1 Pkg 8.5 oz. Jiffy corn muffin mix
- 1/4 cup buttermilk
- 3/4 stick butter, melted
- 1 medium onion, chopped
- 1 10 oz. Pkg frozen chopped spinach - thaw and squeeze out the water
- 3 cups grated cheddar cheese (reserve 1 cup for topping)

In a 10 inch iron skillet, brown the sliced sausage. Remove sausage from pan and set aside. Place skillet in pre-heated oven.

In a large bowl, beat eggs. Add cornbread mix, buttermilk, melted butter, onions, and squeezed spinach. Fold in chopped sausage, and cheese except for (1 cup).

Remove iron skillet from oven. Place mixture in hot skillet and top with remaining cheese.

Bake for 30 minutes or until pick comes out clean.

Note: If you are baking this in a foil pan for a pot luck meal, add 15 minutes to the baking time. - Libby

Lisa Kirkman

JERRY'S EASY OVEN ROUX - CHICKEN GUMBO

Preheat oven to 350 ºF.

- 1 chicken – boiled and picked (keep the liquid)
- broth from chicken – de-fatted
- 2 cups all-purpose flour
- 2 cups olive oil
- 1 large onion, chopped
- 1 large green bell pepper, chopped
- 3 stalks celery, chopped
- 1 32 oz. Pkg frozen okra
- Salt and pepper to taste
- 1 t. sugar
- 2-3 bay leaves
- 2 - 14.5 oz. cans diced tomatoes

In a 10 inch cast iron skillet mix olive oil and flour. Place skillet in the oven for 2 ½ hours stirring the roux every 20 minutes. The color will turn to a peanut butter color, then to a milk chocolate color and finally to a dark chocolate color. At the 2 ½ hour mark (or dark chocolate color) DO NOT stir the roux a final time. Remove the skillet from the oven and carefully pour off any excess oil floating on the top of the roux. You may discard the oil or jar it for seasoning use later in other dishes.

Immediately put your chopped celery, onion and peppers into the hot skillet roux mix. This will cool down and stop the

MEETING AT MATTHEW STREET

cooking of the roux while simultaneously cooking the vegetables. The roux will darken when you add the vegetables.

Scrape the roux into a large pot and add all the remaining ingredients. Boil and season to taste. Do not over dilute with too much broth. It should be thick and not too runny.

Serve over rice.

Note: Leave dishes for someone else to clean. You've done enough for one day. - Jerry

Lisa Kirkman

AMOS'S INDIAN CURRY AND MANGO CHICKEN

- 3 tablespoons olive oil
- 1 small onion, chopped
- 1/2 green bell pepper, chopped
- 2 cloves garlic, minced
- 1 t. grated ginger root
- 1 t. paprika
- 1 t. ground cinnamon
- 3 T. curry powder
- 2 t. Salt
- 1 t. sugar
- 1 t. Garam Masala
- 2 chicken breasts, boneless, no skin, cut into bite-sized pieces
- 1 – 15 oz. bottle of Naked Mango juice
- 1/2 cup pineapple tidbits
- 1/2 T. lemon juiced
- 1 can coconut milk
- 2 bay leaves
- 1 T. tomato paste
- 1 T. coconut extract
- 1 cup plain Greek yogurt (I like Cabots)

Heat olive oil in a large pot over medium heat. Sauté onion and bell pepper until lightly browned. Stir in garlic, and all the spices. Continue stirring for 2 minutes and enjoy the aroma. Add chicken pieces and sauté for a few minutes, then add all remaining ingredients. Bring to a boil, reduce heat, and simmer for 20 to 25 minutes.
Serve over rice.

MEETING AT MATTHEW STREET

Note: Two things, don't let this list of ingredients scare you. It's a one pot meal and extremely simple. The flavor is outstanding and the amazing aroma will linger in the kitchen all day.
Secondly, don't ever get roped into cleaning up after Jerry. He leaves the kitchen an absolute mess! – Amos

Lisa Kirkman

ACKNOWLEDGEMENTS

Phil Kittell – my husband for reading the first chapter after I wrote it and asking me for more.
Alea Kittell – for the cover design (it's also her hand) and finding several corrections that numerous eyes had missed. What an awesome daughter I have! She also took the author photo of me.
Stephanie and Rob Knight – for reading the very first draft and giving me encouragement and solid feedback toward proceeding. I would not have gone further with the book without your positive reaction. And yes, I'll work on Book II.
James Billie – former chief of the Seminole Indian Tribe, for your phone call immediately after reading the manuscript. The first sentence you said to me was awesome! "Where did you get those * words?" I'm glad the message connected with you!
William (Bill) Mize – my date to the senior prom and now author! Thank you for your advice and guidance while I worked through the process of publishing my book. William is the Shamus Award nominated creator of the Denton Ward and Monty Crocetti mystery series.
Derek Hancock – for a sermon about Skubalon – Philippians 3:8. I lay awake one night hoping you'd like my manuscript. The very next day you contacted me with the suggestion to turn it into a series of books. Thanks for putting my mind at ease. I really value your feedback and it was hugely encouraging to get your positive response.
Charles Weissinger – For thinking enough of my manuscript to want to get it into the hands of John Grisham and Greg Iles when I was looking for a literary agent and/or publisher.
Melissa Anderson – my Beta reader, editor and fellow writer. You are an awesome friend! Thank you for your support in so many many ways.

MEETING AT MATTHEW STREET

Michelle and Tom Warren – for making numerous notes, suggestions and corrections to typos…some by accident, and some due to my own ignorance. It's great to have smart neighbors. Also neat to know that the book, Anthem, connected with Michelle like it did with me! Small book – big message!

Mary Lou Hall – for helping me remember the word splagchnizomai from a sermon preached at your church in Elizabethtown, KY in May, 2014

Maureen Valentino – for your editing skills and friendship.

Dr. Jason Kapnick – for becoming a wonderful email pen pal off of whom I could bounce questions. Thank you for your positive support of me. But y'all, my syntax bothered this dear Harvard man. So I told him, "Proper grammar is something up with which I will not put!"

Joshua River – For originally directing me to the meaning of praus.

June Merritt – For her enormous help with the 2nd edition corrections. There was hardly a page her expertise did not touch. She hates the word "that!!" I left several, however, because I felt sorry for the poor little word. Great mentor! Thanks, June!

Beta readers - Jill Grove, Stephanie and Rob Knight, Alea Kittell, Phil Kittell, Melissa Anderson, Lynn Marie Anderson, Rick Hazlip, James Billie, Michelle and Tom Warren, Maureen Valentino, Charles and Anne Weissinger, Margi Baker, Rick and Laura Slone, Glenn Miller, Debbie Waterer, Dr. Jason Kapnick, Liz Kirkman, Brian and Nancy Barr, Derek Hancock, Diane Moore, Charles Pickering, and Chaplain Bryan Crittendon.

The fact that you took the time out of your busy lives to read my manuscript means a lot to me. Believe me! I know the value of free time and how little of it we have. I am humbled by your sharing of that most precious commodity by reading the earliest versions of "Meeting at Matthew Street" and giving me encouragement.

Lisa Kirkman

SOURCE NOTES

https://www.pharocattle.com/wp-content/uploads/html/SundayInspirations/Beatitudes/The_Beatitudes_Part_3_cont_090708.htm
The Beatitude concerning the English word "meek"
http://www.bibleprobe.com/descent.htm - Regarding saints raising from their tombs
https://www.truthortradition.com/articles/what-about-matthew-2752-and-53 - regarding the consistency of the passage over time
https://www.blueletterbible.org/lang/lexicon/lexicon.cfm?t=kjv&strongs=g4697 – defining and pronouncing *splagchnizomai*
https://www.aans.org/Patients/Neurosurgical-Conditions-and-Treatments/Gunshot-Wound-Head-Trauma - head trauma due to gunshot wounds
KILLING JESUS – by Bill O'Reilly and Martin Dugard
https://www.whitehousehistory.org/abraham-lincolns-white-house - Abe Lincoln's White House
https://en.wikipedia.org/wiki/Billy_Graham - Billy Graham's early life
https://www2.wheaton.edu/bgc/archives/GUIDES/048.htm - Youth for Christ Schedule
King James Bible
https://en.wikipedia.org/wiki/Gonzalo_Fern%C3%A1ndez_de_C%C3%B3rdoba – El Gran Captain - Gonzalo Fernandez Cordoba
https://warfarehistorynetwork.com/2016/07/22/gonzalo-de-cordoba-grand-captain-of-renaissance-warfare/ - Cordoba

ABOUT THE AUTHOR

Lisa Kirkman lives in Pensacola, FL with her husband Phillip Kittell. She had been in marketing for a few years before she started her own promotional products company at the age of 26. Within ten months it was so successful that she had to incorporate the business. Over the next 32 years she used her imagination to help her customers successfully promote their own businesses. Ever since the age of 16 she has been hired several times per year as a professional musician, and she had a CD produced by Grammy Award Winning record producer Larry Butler. Currently, she donates her musical talents to her non-denominational church, playing multiple musical instruments in their contemporary Christian band. Over the years she's enjoyed studying the process of fusing glass and became an award winning glass artist. Most evenings she can be found entertaining her dog and a local blue heron by throwing a cast net, bringing all three of them great joy. There's nothing she won't try. And that's why….

"Meeting at Matthew Street" is Lisa's first attempt at writing a novel.

REVIEWS

If you have enjoyed my book, please share it with a friend, or buy an additional copy for a family member.

In addition to that, a review on Goodreads and Amazon would be greatly appreciated. And, if you are BFFs with a book reviewer, call them!

The support of my readers is so awesome. Think about the lives that might be touched by the message that "being praus" conveys. Isn't it a great word? On the back of my car is a bumper sticker which my company made that reads:
I am Praus – I read Meeting at Matthew Street.
Help me make that phrase become recognized worldwide.
Thanks you! - Lisa

Go to www.MeetingAtMatthewStreet.com for I AM PRAUS bumper stickers, t-shirts and more!

MEETING AT MATTHEW STREET

COMING UP

I AM PRAUS!
The continuation of Meeting at Matthew Street

So many of my Beta Readers wanted
Meeting at Matthew Street to continue further.

They longed to find out what was going to happen next!
In book II you'll find out that working in the background was
much safer than being discovered and out in the open...
that's true for both the twelve elect AND Viktor Hoven!

Find out who comes forward to declare...
I AM PRAUS!

Made in the USA
Columbia, SC
31 March 2021